B'RATS TALES

The Refuge Adventure

by
Lucy Moreland

Illustrated by
Robin Apple

TEXALINA PRESS

TEXAS

ARKANSAS

TEXALINA PRESS

TEXAS

ARKANSAS

ROXTON, TEXAS
MAUMELLE, ARKANSAS

This book is a work of fiction. References to real people, events, establishments, organizations, or locales are intended only to provide a sense of authenticity and are used to advance the fictional narrative. All characters, human or anthropomorphic, are drawn from the author's imagination and are not meant to be construed as real or based on any individual, living or dead.

ISBN: 0692849637

ISBN-13: 978-0692849637

Printed in the United States of America

Texalina Press

To Myah, Anna, Nate and Ashley

May your adventures be fun and your dreams come true.

--Honey

Contents

Chapter One
Trapped Like a Rat

As the street clock chimed midnight in the riverside city, the creatures of the night scurried from place to place looking for morsels of food to sustain them another day. Behind Fipple's Fresh Fish Market, a small shadow scuttled about in the dimly lit alley. Cautiously watching for danger, the small, furry, male **rodent**[1] enjoyed a feast of cake and cookie crumbs discarded from the bakery located next to the fish market. While munching on his tasty meal, the ambitious little mouse remained constantly on the alert. Hungry cats always patrolled the alley.

While the mouse scampered about the alley, he did not realize danger lurked under the rusted stairs leading to the back door of the bakery. Two cold, green eyes followed every move the creature made.

The ragged old alley cat's muscles tensed at the thought of a mouse for dinner. The hungry tomcat could hardly endure the anticipation. Its only movement, a twitch at the end of his tail, indicated the tomcat's concentration on its unsuspecting victim. As the mouse moved closer and closer, the cat crouched lower and lower, readying to pounce at the right—

Suddenly, like a bolt of lightning, the cat sprung from his dark corner anxiously expecting to ambush the tiny mouse. With his eyes

[1] Rodent – A mammal with large orange teeth that constantly grow. *Example: Beavers, squirrels, rats and mice are all rodents.*

1

fixed on his **prey**[2], the shabby cat bounded in front of the mouse and, with his sharp claws fully extended, took a mighty swing at his victim.

Although the cat expected to easily grab his game, his claws only grazed the mouse's head as it leapt for its life. Bounding around and beneath trash in the filthy alley, the mouse raced toward a garbage can hoping for safety, the cat in close pursuit. As the mouse spun around the corner and jumped into a garbage can filled with old newspapers and books, he felt the vibrations of the cat's large paws from behind. Digging and chewing his way through the waste paper, the agile mouse dug its way to safety in the center of the can. The large feline pawed the top of the can and growled, disgusted and defeated.

Even though the close encounter left the mouse breathless, he kept chewing and digging through the bundles of newspapers and magazines as it sought safety in the bottom of the can.

When reaching the last layer of papers, the mouse heard a noise from the bottom of the can.

Could it be another mouse? It sounded like another mouse. Maybe another mouse had escaped from the cats.

Anticipating meeting a new friend, the mouse chewed faster and faster. Finally, as the last layer of paper fell to the bottom of the can, the mouse poked his head through a small hole. Looking back, whisker to whisker, nose to nose, and eye to eye sat the biggest, ugliest rat the mouse had ever seen.

The two rodents stared at each other in shock, until the cocky rat raised its eyebrows and very sternly asked, "What are you doing in my trash can? Get out, and get out now."

"I'm sorry I bothered you. I didn't mean to intrude into your home," the shiny-eyed rodent answered. "I'll leave just as soon as I can. A tomcat chased me down the alley, and this trash can was the only safe place I could find."

The mouse seemed to fear the rat as much as the tomcat.

"Just show me the way out, and I will leave," it timidly added. "That giant, old cat out there has a bad attitude."

"There's the door," said the rat, pointing to another hole rusted

---

[2] **Prey** – Animals that are normally eaten by other animals. *Example: The cat is a predator, and the mouse is its prey.*

through the old garbage can.

The mouse approached the dimly lit hole, but the alley cat swung its paw inside, pinning the resident rat's body to the floor. Without hesitating, the mouse ran to aid the helpless rat.

"Bite the cat!" the rat shouted.

When the mouse bit down on the paw of the cat, the intruder squalled with pain, and the rat escaped its grasp.

"Yuck… Poooeee," gagged the little mouse. "That is a foul-tasting cat."

"Well, just how many cats have you tasted?" the rat asked with a smirk.

"Oh, I've chewed a few paws and cat tails in my time," the mouse boasted.

With bruised pride and a slight limp, the tomcat dragged his tail down the alley in search of a fish carcass to satisfy his hunger pains.

"Considering you helped me outwit that cat, I guess you can stay the night," snapped the pompous rat. "But don't think you're moving in."

"If you'll let me spend the night, I'll be glad to leave in the morning," murmured the mouse as it ducked his head into a corner of the tiny room.

"My name is Malachi. What's yours?" asked the mouse.

"What do you mean, what's my name? I don't believe I have one," the rat said. "But if I wanted a name, I could get one."

"You mean your mother didn't name you when you were a baby? I thought everyone had a name," said Malachi. "Well, I'll just have to name you. What would you like to be called?"

"Well, I never gave it much thought," the rat answered. "I've been called all kinds of names, but none ever stuck. What would be a good name for me?"

"I don't know. I've never named anyone before," said the young mouse. "I'll have to give it some thought."

"Well, how did you get your name, Malachi?" asked the rat.

"I was born in the back of the church library," Malachi answered. "My mother made a bed of paper from some of the books in the library, and I always slept on a page with the word 'Malachi' printed on it. It

sounded like a boy's name, so all my brothers and sisters called me Malachi."

Excited at the thought of having a name of his own, the rat ripped the newspaper from the floor of his garbage can home.

"Read this, and give me a name," he demanded. "I've slept in this old can for a few days. Is my name on this sheet of paper?"

"I don't know which word to call you," the mouse said as he scanned the scrap of newspaper. "I'll tell you what. I'm going to start reading, and if you like a particular word, stop me. That word will be your name."

"Be sure it's a boy's name," the rat grumbled.

As Malachi moved over to the hole in the can, the dim streetlights shown on the paper covered with words. He began reading from the torn newspaper:

> *"located in the south, the wildlife will have improved **habitat**³ for animals that are now considered over-populated in one specific area. A cougar..."*

"Stop," the rat said abruptly. "I like that word—'Cougar.' It sounds like a fine, manly name for a city rat."

"You have no idea what 'cougar' means," snapped the mouse.

"I don't care what it means," said the rat." I like the word, and that is what I want to be called—'cougar'."

"Okay," said Malachi. "But you sure don't look like a large cat."

"I'm not a cat. I'm a rat," he spouted. Malachi strutted toward the rat, grabbed his irritating landlord by the whiskers, and pulled his head close enough to whisper in his ear.

"A cougar is a very, very, very, large, ferocious, mean cat," he said. "And cougars eat very, very, very, little, obnoxious rats. So, for that fact

---

³ **Habitat** – The natural homes of plants and animals. There are a number of different types of habitats. A forest, a wetland, a meadow, an ocean, and a desert are all different habitats. *Example: A cactus lives in the hot, dry desert.*

and that fact alone, I will not call you 'Cougar'."

"No problem," the rat said with a gulp. "Keep reading, but turn the paper over. I don't want to hear anything else about cougars."

Malachi found many of words on the back side of the paper torn in half. He couldn't make them sound right.

> *"mental hazards are sweeping th*
> *arge city streets at an alarming rate.*
> *nty health department has advised tha*
> *b rats and mice ..."*

"Stop," the rat shouted. "That's it right there. That's my name."

"What's *it?*" asked Malachi.

"I want to be called B'rats," said the enthusiastic rat. "And don't tell me that a 'D'rat' is a cat. It says 'R-A-T' in the letters, and that is what I am—a rat. And a handsome rat, I might add."

As the rat pranced about the room shouting his new name, Malachi sat down on the floor and scratched his head. Is B'rats an appropriate name for an arrogant rat?

"Yes, you are a rat alright," Malachi said. "You're a rat from the tip of your ears to the end of your ratty little tail, and I can't think of a better name for you. B'rats it is."

Excited about his new name, B'rats encouraged Malachi to read more about the drats and mice.

"Let me see. Where was I?" mumbled Malachi.

> *"b rats and mice are becoming a health*
> *hazard to humans and **eradication**[4] of*
> *the nuisance rodents is encouraged.*

"Oh, no," exclaimed Malachi. "Do you know what this means, B'rats?"

"Let me guess. Maybe I should have picked 'eradication' instead of B'rats," the rat sarcastically replied.

[4] **Eradication**- To completely do away with; "get rid of." *Example: The plant was eradicated by pulling it up by the roots.*

Again, Malachi grabbed the rat's whiskers and whispered in his ear, "Do you know what 'eradication' means?"

"Well, excuse me for being so stupid," B'rats said. "No, I don't know what eradication means. It sounds important and I—"

"It means to kill, do away with, eliminate," Malachi said. "Do rat-traps ring a bell to you? Do you get the picture?"

"Yes, I do," said B'rats. "And if you grab my whiskers one more time, I'm going to throw you out of this can and let a cougar eradicate you."

"Oh, hush and listen," ordered Malachi. "We've got big problems. Not only do we have cats to contend with, we have humans to deal with too. We're talking 'Mouse Trap City'. They're after us, and we have to figure out how to get out of this town."

As the two rodents paced the floor, Malachi again turned over the paper with the words written on it. He began reading the other side.

> *"Cougars, eagles, bears, and animals of*
> *all sizes will find a **refuge**⁵ in the south.*
> *There will be a total of 95,000 acres of*
> *perfect habitat dedicated to wildlife."*

"That's it," Malachi said. "We'll head south to this wildlife refuge. We'll leave first thing in the morning."

"Now, wait just a minute," said B'rats, "What is this 'we' stuff? I haven't agreed to go anywhere. How do you plan to find this refuge anyhow? Are you going to call a cab to come get us? Or are we flying down south?"

Malachi raised his eyebrow and leaned toward the egotistical four-footed rodent. B'rats jumped back and covered his whiskers.

"Don't even think about grabbing my whiskers," he warned.

"You're a good student, B'rats," Malachi said. "And you're the first friend I've found in this city. Even though you are a pain in a rat's tail, I would never forgive myself if I left you here to get smacked in a rattrap.

You're going with me to a land where there are no dirty alleys,

⁵ **Refuge**- A place of safety, particularly for something or someone in danger. *Example: The deer found refuge from predators in the middle of the forest.*

7

no stinky cars, no old garbage cans with rotten food and drinks, and none of the other dangers of city life," he added. "We are going to the woods."

"I don't think so," snorted B'rats. "As I recall, you're the mouse who rudely grabbed my whiskers and told me about the cougars living in the woods. You know—those very, very, very big cats that eat very, very, very small rats?"

"Cougars will not be a problem," Malachi stated.

"And, O' Intelligent One, how do you know they will not be a problem?" asked B'rats.

"According to this newspaper article," Malachi explained, "the cougar is an **endangered species**[6], and there aren't many left because humans have eradicated them—the same humans who want to eradicate rats and mice in this city. Now are you going with me or not?"

"I don't know," replied B'rats. "I'll let you know in the morning. I'm tired, and I want to go to sleep now. You can make your bed over there in the corner."

"Thank you very much," said Malachi.

As the two rodents settled in for the night, a pleasant smile spread over their faces. Malachi had found a friend, and B'rats was the proud owner of a new name.

After Malachi fell asleep, B'rats rolled over and picked up the newsprint with his name on it. He neatly rolled up the ragged piece of paper, placed it under his head, closed his eyes, and went to sleep.

[6] **Endangered Species**- A group of animals in danger of extinction if not protected. *Example: American Bald Eagles were once an endangered species because few remained in the wild.*

NOTES

NOTES

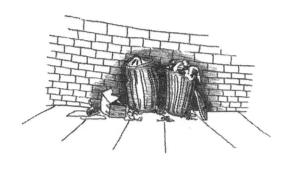

Chapter Two
Dumped and Stuffed

A blanket of **fog**[7] settled on the river the next morning, but the sounds of a busy city coming to life disturbed the two sleeping rodents. They found the banging metal trashcans especially annoying. The racket soon approached the can housing Malachi and B'rats.

Suddenly B'rats jumped up, grabbed Malachi by the tail, and yanked him through the rusty trashcan's make-shift-door. Before Malachi could say a word, he sat in the street behind an old brick.

"What in the world are you—?"

B'rats had wrapped his tail around Malachi's **muzzle**[8].

"Hush. It's the trash people," growled B'rats. "These greedy people always take my belongings. My house, my food—they leave me nothing, and I have to start collecting food and building a new home."

Malachi sat stunned.

"Oh, no" cried B'rats. "My name. My name. They'll get my name! I have to get my name out of that can before they put it on that big truck."

B'rats bolted from his hiding place behind the brick, racing to beat the man to his trashcan. Just as the man picked up the can, B'rats dived into the rusted hole. Again, Malachi sat stunned. The man lifted

---

[7] **Fog** - A thick cloud formed by tiny water droplets, or water vapor, near the earth's surface. *Example: The fog was so thick we could not see the trees.*

[8] **Muzzle** – The extended jaw and nose of an animal. *Example: The dog has a long muzzle.*

both B'rats and his home into the
air and dumped them in a large
truck. Malachi thought of the
newspaper he read the night before. *'Eradication.'* He knew he
had to save B'rats.

As the truck moved to the
next group of trash cans, Malachi
noticed a rope hanging behind
the area B'rats and his home
had been dumped. With a burst
of mouse speed, he chased after the truck, jumped and clung
to the rope, climbed to the trash
container, and hid in a small veg-
etable can.

Paper, plastic, glass, and metal containers crashed down on Malachi as the man emptied the last can on the street.

Soon the truck stopped, and the engine fell quiet. Two men left and
went inside the bakery. Now was Malachi's chance.

He began digging and calling for B'rats. Frantically chewing
through papers, Malachi would pause only long enough to listen for
B'rats.

A sudden movement on the other side of the truck attracted Malachi's attention. It was the end of B'rats' tail. Malachi ran to it and jerked
on the skinny slightly furred tail. Out popped B'rats.

"Boy, am I glad to see you," spouted B'rats. "Now you can help me
look for my name."

"Have you lost your mind?" snapped Malachi.

"No, I have lost my name," shouted the upset rat.

"You haven't lost your name. All you have lost is a ragged, old piece
of paper with your name written on it. You will always have your name.
That is one thing nobody can take away from you," said Malachi.

"I don't care," said B'rats. "I want that piece of ragged, old paper.
It's mine, and I am going to look for it with or without your help"

B'rats jumped into the heap of **rubbish**[9], but not before Malachi grabbed his tail and bit down hard on its end.

B'rats shot straight up out of the garbage and screamed with pain.

"Ouch. Are you hungry or just plain crazy?" shouted B'rats.

"Neither," said Malachi. "You've got to listen to me, and listen to me now. Do you know what this machine is that we are riding in?"

"Yes, indeed I do," said B'rats. "It's a restaurant on wheels. Just look at all the food. This is my new mobile home, my own personal restaurant, and I'm willing to share it with you if you'll quit biting my tail and help me find my name."

"We don't have time for this," said Malachi. "Not only is this a traveling food bin, it is also a rodent eradication truck. Look up there at those big doors. When those men come back, they're going to slam those doors shut and squash us. I've seen it happen before."

"You've seen rats and mice squashed?" asked B'rats, skeptically.

"No, I've not seen them squashed," Malachi said. "I've just seen the doors shut, and the mice and rats inside never return."

"Ughhh," gasped B'rats. "The men are coming, and there is nowhere to hide. Tell me what to do, Malachi."

"Follow me."

The two little rodents climbed to the top of the garbage heap, grabbed a metal bar at the top of the truck, and wiggled into an old bottle.

"This should be a safe place for a while," said Malachi. "When the truck stops again, we'll just have to get off and find our way to that refuge we read about last night."

As B'rats and Malachi rode in the bumpy garbage truck, Malachi read the passing street signs. All of the signs said south. First, there was "South Maple Street" then "South Elm Street," and the last road was "South Oak Street." The little mouse wondered if the truck might be taking them south, close to the refuge he had read about the night before.

Malachi poked his head out of the old bottle. He saw a beautiful blue river to the left; and to the right he saw a row of docks and warehouses. The

---

[9] **Rubbish** - Waste material and trash. *Example: The garbage truck was filled with rubbish from the city.*

truck began to slow down as it traveled along the rough road. It suddenly came to a complete stop and began to back onto a large **barge**[10] docked in the river.

"They couldn't squash us, so now they're going to drown us," shouted B'rats.

"Listen to me," said Malachi. "Remember the story I read to you last night? Didn't it say that the animal refuge was in the south?"

"Yes, I think so," said B'rats. "But that is not what I am worried about now. Drowning is my main concern."

"Can you see which way the river is flowing?" asked Malachi.

B'rats picked up Malachi by the nape of his neck and looked him straight in the eyes.

"Malachi, it's time to focus on our problem," he said calmly. "Focus…. Focus…. Focus. We're going to be fish bait if you don't get a grip, and it won't matter which way the river is flowing. If we drown, we'll be dead, and we'll just float wherever it does," shouted the hysterical rat.

Malachi reached over and once again grabbed the out-of-control rat by the whiskers.

"We're not going to drown," he said. "We're going to ride the garbage barge south with the river to the animal refuge. First, we have to get out of this bottle. Follow me."

Malachi got a running start and popped out of the bottle.

"Come on, and be quick about it. We don't have much time."

B'rats scrambled to the top of the bottle and poked his head out, but he could the rest of his body remained inside.

"Grrrrr, Grrrrr," groaned the fat rat as he tried to squirm his way through the opening.

"What is wrong with you now?" Malachi asked disgustedly.

"I'm stuck," the rat groaned.

"You're stuck?" Seriously? asked Malachi. "You went in to that bottle, so you should be able to come out of that bottle too."

Malachi frowned and scolded B'rats, then impatiently ran up to the

[10] **Barge** - A large flat-bottomed boat with tall sides that carries freight and is most often pushed by a tugboat. *Example: The tugboat pushed the trash-loaded barge down the river.*

bottle, positioned his two tiny feet on either side of its top, and grabbed B'rats' whiskers. He began to pull. B'rats became very angry about having his whiskers pulled.

"I'm sorry, B'rats, but this is the only way to get you out," Malachi said.

When large tears formed in the rat's eyes, Malachi realized his friend was really stuck. If whisker pulling would not get B'rats out, only one thing could.

"Back up, B'rats," ordered Malachi. "I need to push you out of this mess you are in."

B'rats backed into the bottom of the bottle, and Malachi wiggled easily through its top.

"Now," instructed Malachi, "stick your head through the hole, and I will push you out."

Malachi began pushing, working to release B'rats from his glass prison.

"It's no use," fussed the rat. "I'll just be buried in a mountain of trash in this glass coffin."

"Oh, no. You will not," snapped the tiny mouse as he clicked his teeth together. Malachi gripped B'rats tail tightly and bit it right on the end.

"Yaowwww," screamed the rat.

Like a bullet, B'rats exploded out of the bottle, with Malachi attached to his tail. The two rodents sailed over the tall side of the truck, landing in the middle of the garbage barge.

Dazed after their crash landing, Malachi and B'rats could only stare at each other. However, when the garbage truck started dumping its load of trash, B'rats and Malachi ran toward the back of the barge. Before they had taken three steps, something grabbed them by their tails and stuffed them into a dark soft pocket-shaped pouch. They heard a high-pitched frantic voice.

"You youngsters get over here before you are covered with garbage."

Before Malachi and B'rats could catch their breath, two more furry creatures abruptly arrived inside the pocket. Before long, many mouse-sized animals were diving into the increasingly crowded pouch.

As Malachi and B'rats huddled in a corner of the pouch, they couldn't figure out what had caught them, where they were, and even more so, what would become of them. Through the darkness, they could see six strange-looking rats huddled on the other side of the pouch.

"I believe it is time for us to get out of here, B'rats," whispered Malachi.

The two prisoners climbed to the top of the pouch and looked up at the biggest rat they had ever seen in their lives. This animal stood more than a foot tall and had a five-inch whisker spread. Malachi and B'rats looked at each other, swallowed hard, and bounded from the top of the pouch. In seconds, the giant rat whisked them up by their tails and stuffed them back inside.

"Now you get in there, and stay in there until I say it's safe to come out," scolded the large animal.

"Well, what now?" whispered B'rats.

"I guess we will stay in here until 'IT' is ready for us to come out," muttered Malachi.

"That's right," sneered a voice from across the pouch. "Mama will pluck you bald if you don't listen to her."

"There isn't anybody who's going to pluck me bald," boasted B'rats as he bullied his way to the middle of the pocket.

As B'rats burst across the pouch, the six shuddering babies fainted dead away.

"B'rats, you scared those little fellows to death," said Malachi.

"They aren't even breathing. Look at them. They're as limp as rags."

"I-I-I d-d-didn't mean to scare them to death," stuttered B'rats.

"Well, you better do something fast because Mama just gave the 'all-clear,' and she is expecting her youngsters to come out and play," whispered Malachi.

"Are you going to hurt us?" whimpered a timid voice from the corner.

"You're alive," B'rats gasped.

"Of course, we're alive," mumbled another small voice. "Don't you know about playing-possum?"

"What is playing-possum?" asked B'rats.

"Playing-possum is what an **opossum**[11] does when there is danger," explained one of the little animals. "All you have to do to play is to lay on your side and be very, very still. When the danger passes, you get up and run away."

Malachi and B'rats suddenly realized a giant rat wasn't holding them captive; rather, it was an opossum.

Mother opossum soon opened the pouch.

"Everybody out and find your dinner," she said.

All the little opossums jumped out of the pouch and scrambled around digging in the fresh garbage dumped from the truck.

B'rats and Malachi remained in the pouch and wondered how they would get out of their predicament without Mother opossum finding them.

"Let's just go for it," said B'rats.

"One-two-three… Go," said Malachi, and both rodents jumped from Mother opossum's pouch. When they landed, all of the little opossums chased and tried to play with them. Mother opossum waddled

---

[11] **Opossum** –A nocturnal mammal (normally active at night) with a pointed snout and prehensile tail capable of grasping objects. *Example: The grey and white opossum wrapped its tail around the limb to keep from falling out of the tree.*

over to Malachi and B'rats and firmly placed her foot on their tails. Immediately, B'rats fell over on his side and held his breath.

"Mama, Mama," cried the little opossums. "They won't hurt us."

"They are our friends," shouted one of the little opossums.

"What were you doing in my pouch?" growled mother opossum.

"You put us in there by mistake when the truck dumped the trash," said Malachi. "I guess you thought we were two of your babies. In fact, B'rats and I were just discussing what a fine group of youngsters you have. Weren't we, B'rats? B'rats? B'rats?"

"What is wrong with the rat?" asked the large opossum.

"I don't know. He was fine just a few minutes ago," exclaimed Malachi.

Malachi leaned over B'rats and began slapping him on the head and pulling his whiskers.

"B'rats, what's wrong with you?"

B'rats opened one eye, winked at Malachi, and whispered, "I'm playing possum."

"Get up from there. You're a rat, not an opossum," spouted Malachi. B'rats jumped up and looked into the shiny black eyes of the large opossum.

"You look like a rat, you eat like a rat, and you have lots of little rat-looking babies. Why are you not a rat?" he asked.

"Because I am an opossum. Priscilla O. Possum is my name, but you can call me Prissy. I am a **marsupial**[12], and I have a pouch to prove it.

B'rats patted his stomach in search of a pouch.

"You, my dear rat, are a rodent. Your teeth grow all the time, so that makes you a rodent," explained the informed opossum.

"I knew that," sneered B'rats. "Let's get out of here, Malachi. Let's find the refuge. I'm tired of being chased, dumped, stuck, stuffed, and bit. My whiskers are so sore I can't even snarl. Let's go."

While the dockworkers untied the massive, cumbersome ropes holding the barge in place, the loud roar of a diesel engine sounded

---

[12] **Marsupial** - A group of animals that have pouches where young are raised. *Example: A Kangaroo and an opossum are both types of marsupials.*

from upstream. Soon the enormous heap of garbage drifted freely in the river. A tugboat attached itself to the giant barge and pushed it into the channel. The two tiny passengers had reached the point of no return.

Like sailors going to sea, B'rats and Malachi enjoyed the scenery and excitement of their adventure and search for a safe new home. With all the food they could possibly eat and no alley cats on board, the two shipmates kicked back and enjoyed the sun and the rocking motion of the waves.

NOTES

Chapter Three
Overboard

As the belching diesel tugboat pushed the garbage-filled barges through the river valley, the two rodents looked in awe at the scenic granite bluffs on the east side of the river and to the west at beautiful **delta**[13] farmland. After two days, B'rats and Malachi set forth for a new way of life, free from alley cats and other **predators**[14].

The mid-day sun beat down on the barge, and Malachi noticed large storm clouds building to the southwest. Lightning flashed in the distance, and the sound of thunder rolled across the mountains and fields. Soon the waves along the river began to **whitecap**[15], and the barges tossed about on the once peaceful water. The men on the tugboat jumped from barge to barge and secured ropes and cables to ensure the barges wouldn't break free and escape the control of the tugboat.

The rain began falling from the sky like water poured from a bucket. Malachi and B'rats huddled in a large, white foam cup to escape the wind and rain. The wind grew stronger, and the waves began spilling onto

---

[13] **Delta**- A track of land that is formed by the sediment deposited by a river. *Example: The farmer planted crops in the rich soil deposited by the river.*

[14] **Predator** – An animal that kills and eats other animals. *Example: The snake, a predator, caught and ate the mouse.*

[15] **Whitecap** – small waves with a foamy white crest. *Example: The high winds blowing across a lake caused waves to have whitecaps.*

the barge. The mighty tug had a terrible time controlling the barges, as its crew fought to navigate the narrow river channel.

All at once, the two little rodents found themselves thrown from their cup as a loud crash sounded. The tug's engine had stalled. Some of the barges and the tug had become stuck on a **sandbar**[16] at the river's edge. In fact, the only barge that was moving had broken free from the others and floated down the river out of control. It just so happened to be the very barge Malachi and B'rats had been riding. The two rodents ran to the corner of the barge and found dry shelter in an old cardboard box.

As the renegade barge floated sideways down the choppy river, Malachi saw an old railroad bridge directly in its path. As the barge sped faster and faster downstream and whipped out of control, the two stowaways could only brace themselves for the unavoidable collision about to take place.

"Hold on B'rats," shouted Malachi.

A loud and enormous crunch sounded as the barge rammed into the huge concrete supports of the bridge. The impact sent Malachi and B'rats overboard into the turbulent, cold river. A deluge of garbage and trash accompanied the two rodents into the water. Malachi and B'rats could not control their fate as they tossed about the raging river like feathers in a whirlwind.

The friends became separated and unsure if they would ever see each other again, let alone survive. B'rats desperately tried to climb atop the pile of **debris**[17] that had fallen into the river when the barge hit the bridge. He found the bottles too slippery to climb upon, and the cans sank from his weight.

Suddenly, a bright, pink, foam egg carton floated alongside B'rats. The cold wet creature managed to climb onto the makeshift raft and scanned the choppy water for his friend Malachi.

[16] **Sandbar** – A ridge of sand and sedimentation deposited in a body of water by movement and settlement (i.e., currents in a river). *Example: The shore birds searched for minnows on the edge of the sandbar.*

[17] **Debris** – Trash; broken or discarded items often resulting from a natural disaster. *Example: After the storm, the ground was littered with debris.*

In the distance, B'rats heard a weak voice calling his name.

"B'rats, D'r-a-a-a-a-t-t-s? Where are you, B'rats?"

It was Malachi. B'rats saw his buddy floating on a garbage bag filled with trash and a pocket of air. As the wind caught the bag, it pushed the little mouse closer and closer to B'rats. When he was within jumping range, Malachi bailed off the garbage bag and landed in the middle of B'rats and his floating egg carton.

"Oh, B'rats, I thought you were fish bait. Gone forever," shouted Malachi as he hugged the wet rat.

"We're not out of this yet," B'rats said. "We've got to get to shore before we do become fish bait. Use your tail as a **rudder**[18], and guide this boat to shore."

"Good idea, B'rats. Maybe we will make it after all," cried the wet, little mouse. The two mariners successfully guided their makeshift boat to shore, just as the storm clouds gave way to a beautiful sunset. When the sun disappeared beneath the horizon, it left a sky of evening stars and bright full moon that cast alien shadows frightening the tired adventurers.

"I'm tired, Malachi," groaned B'rats. "Let's find a place to dry off and sleep."

A moonbeam guided the two weary rodents through the vines and dense **underbrush**[19] until they came to a small trail.

"Which way now, Malachi?" moaned the tired rat.

Malachi scratched his tired, little head and looked up at the moon.

"This is south, the way to the refuge," said Malachi as he pointed.

"How do you know which way is south?" challenged B'rats. "It is pitch dark out here, there is no river, and the sun is on the other side of the world."

"Where is the moon, B'rats?" snapped Malachi.

"Over there in the sky," said B'rats.

[18] **Rudder**- an object used to steer a ship or boat. *Example: The boat paddles at the back of the boat was used to steer the boat away from danger.*

[19] **Underbrush** – Vines, bushes, or small trees growing beneath large trees in the forest. *Example: It was hard to walk through the forest because the underbrush was so thick.*

"And which direction does the moon rise?"

B'rats paused a moment.

"Oh, I get it. It rises in the east, so that means this direction is south."

B'rats grinned at his newfound intelligence.

The two explorers followed the trail until coming to a large hollow tree, which had blown over during the afternoon storm and blocked their way. Like many trees, this one had had served as a home for many animals in the forest.

As B'rats and Malachi cautiously explored the tree, they found an abandoned nest on the top limbs. The size of a leaf nest suggested a mother squirrel had raised a large **litter**[20] of babies last fall.

As they scurried down the outside of the hollow trunk, Malachi suddenly disappeared totally out of sight.

"B'rats? D'ra-a-a-ats?" echoed a voice from the center of the tree trunk.

[20] **Litter** – Numerous baby animals born at one time. *Example: My cat had a litter of kittens yesterday.*

"Malachi, where did you go?" yelled B'rats.

"Down here," answered Malachi.

Malachi had fallen into an abandoned woodpecker nest. B'rats ran over to the hole and leaned his head inside. About the same time, Malachi popped out, terrifying B'rats.

"Don't do that anymore," screamed a frightened B'rats.

The two rodents bounced along the log for a few minutes, enjoying their newfound playground. When Malachi jumped to the ground, he landed near something that startled and greatly concerned him.

"Oh, my, B'rats," shouted Malachi. "We've got to get out of here fast. You see this?" Malachi pointed to the ground."

"It looks like fur and bones in a little ball. What is it, Malachi?" asked B'rats.

"It's awful, just awful," Malachi said. "I-It-It's an owl pellet! Hurry. Let's get in this hole and hide."

The two quivering animals ran to the base of the uprooted tree. They found a large opening leading to the center of the hollow trunk.

"Get under these leaves, and be very still, B'rats," whispered Malachi.

"But why? Why are you so upset?" asked B'rats. "You saw bones in the garbage back in the city. You didn't get upset then."

"I've heard about what I just saw, but I've never seen it before, and I hope I never see it again," said Malachi with a shudder. "The bones we saw in the garbage can were chicken bones and steak bones. But these are ow-ow-ow-owl pellets."

"What is an owl pellet, Malachi?" questioned B'rats.

"I just don't even want to think about it," said Malachi, trembling. But B'rats persisted.

"Okay. I'll try to explain it to you, B'rats," started Malachi. "Owls are big birds with sharp claws called talons, and they have very powerful and sharp beaks. Their favorite foods are rodents, particularly mice....and rats."

"Uhoooooo," shivered B'rats.

"These big birds not only eat rats and mice, th....th....they—regurgitate."

"What does regurgitate mean?" asked B'rats.

"It means they throw up the skeletons and fur of rats and mice," whispered Malachi. "You know. Like vomit."

"Sick, Sick, Sick. That is just plain sick," shouted B'rats. "Do you think an owl is here now?"

"Probably not," Malachi reassured B'rats. "Its home was destroyed in the storm, so it's likely looking for a new hollow tree where it can sleep. We should be safe here until morning. Let's try to get some sleep and get an early start. But first, we can eat these mushrooms growing on the side of the tree trunk."

Malachi and B'rats each grabbed a mushroom and began to nibble on its edge.

"What is that awful smell?" asked B'rats.

"Don't look at me; I've just had the longest bath of my life. I've never been so clean," announced Malachi. "But you're right. There is a terrible stench in this old log."

"Well, really, I'm truly insulted."

The slow, southern voice coming from the other end of the log startled Malachi and B'rats, and they crawled all over each other trying to escape whatever had spoken. They envisioned nothing but owls and owl pellets.

"Where are your manners? First, you frighten me with talk about bones and fur then you insult my perfume. Shame on you," remarked the soft-spoken, shiny-eyed creature.

"Wh-Who are you?" asked Malachi.

"My name is Ms. P. U. Skunk, but my friends call me Pooey U, or Pooey for short."

"You're a skunk?" asked Malachi.

"Yes, and a gorgeous one, I might add," Pooey said. "There isn't another skunk in the forest with such beautiful white stripes running from the top of its head to the end of its tail, do you not think?"

Pooey stroked her long beautiful fur.

B'rats leaned over and whispered to Malachi, "Her fur looks like cat fur to me."

"Well Ms. Pooey, just what do skunks eat when they get hungry?" B'rats questioned, cautiously.

"Well it's obvious that you are city rodents who have never seen

an animal like me before," Pooey answered. "Don't worry. I'm not hungry enough to eat a rodent yet. I like insects, earthworms, fruit, and eggs. Oh, how I just love eggs. They make my fur shiny and beautiful."

The sassy southern skunk smirked as she continued to caress her fur and swish her tail from side to side.

"Pooey, you sure do stink," remarked B'rats.

"That's exactly what my mother said when I was born. So she named me Pooey U Stink."

As Pooey stretched and yawned, she stroked her fur and strolled to the end of the hollow log.

"I'll see you boys around," Ms. Pooey said. "I have to go feed my little skunks in my home near the farm. By the way, be careful. That old owl is close-by. If it had not been for this downed tree, that big, old horned owl would have had me for dinner this evening. I ran inside here in the nick of time."

"As bad as you smell, Pooey, I can't imagine anything eating you," remarked Malachi.

"Silly boy, owls can't smell. They would consider a skunk a delicacy if they could only catch one. Skunks are not only beautiful; we are quite intelligent as well," boasted the sleek black and white animal.

Pooey paraded to the end of the hollow log and waved good-bye to the boys. Malachi and B'rats poked their heads through knotholes in the log and took deep breaths as they choked for some fresh air. Soon, they settled down for a good night's rest.

NOTES

Chapter Four
Raccoon Chaos

As the sun began rising over the tall cypress trees, the misty air filled with the sounds of creatures preparing for another busy day. A majestic white-tailed deer cautiously drank its fill of water at the littered riverbank before making its way into the **thicket**[21] to bed down for the day. Agile squirrels leaped from branch to branch, excited about a warm new day. The handsome red-winged blackbirds perched on tall grasses and swayed gracefully in the breeze as they called to their mates.

While the rest of the world awakened, B'rats and Malachi nestled in the leaves of the old, hollow swamp oak the storm had blown down the day before. Suddenly, strange noises tore them from sleep.

B'rats and Malachi jumped from their cozy nest to see what was causing all the commotion. It sounded as if someone was kicking cans and plastic bottles.

Peeping out of the knotholes, the two sleepy-eyed travelers observed a fairyland scene. The heavy dew glistened on the **Spanish moss**[22] elegantly draped from the limbs of the towering cypress trees. Sunrays danced through the majestic bottomland hardwood trees,

[21] **Thicket** – A very dense growth of shrubs, brush, and vines. *Example: The thicket was so dense a rabbit could barely find a way inside.*

[22] **Spanish Moss** – A delicate string-like plant that hangs from tree limbs; primarily found in humid areas of the Southern United States. *Example: Curtains of gray and green Spanish moss draped from the tall trees.*

spotlighting the delicate ferns and May apples. The beautiful feathered jewels of the forest flew from branch to branch searching for the first meal of the day.

Peeping through the knotholes in the downed log, the beauty of nature astounded Malachi and B'rats. But those sounds...

The noise was coming from the riverbank. The two little rodents looked down the small trail they'd traveled the night before. At the river's edge, they could see debris from the barge wreck. Cans, bottles, paper, and plastic littered the shore of the once clean and beautiful river.

B'rats and Malachi heard chattering and the pitiful crying of what sounded like a small animal. Cautiously and quietly, the two curious rodents left their shelter and slipped down the narrow trail where they saw a young grey and black animal struggling with a can and bottle. The animal appeared to have a sharp lid to a can stuck on one front paw and a plastic bottle jammed on the other.

"What is that?" asked B'rats.

"It's a **raccoon**[23], and she's in trouble," said Malachi. "The trash that fell off the barge with us yesterday washed to shore. That nosey raccoon just had to see if there was something in the bottom of that can. The lid must have fallen down on her paw and now she is stuck. Let's help her. She's bleeding."

"Wait just a minute," B'rats interjected. "Before I go out there and help that raccoon, I want to know what a raccoon eats."

"Why are you so worried about what skunks and raccoons eat?" asked Malachi.

"Because I want to know if rodents are on their menus," snorted B'rats. "I didn't come this far to wind up as some strange animal's dinner."

"Oh, quit worrying. You'd probably taste bad anyway," snapped Malachi.

As Malachi and B'rats carefully slipped closer, the raccoon con-

---

[23] **Raccoon** – A raccoon is a medium sized, chunky bodied mammal with five to seven black rings around its tail. It appears as if it has a black mask over its eyes. *Example: The raccoon was in the water searching for fish with its very sensitive front paws.*

tinued to clang and bang as she tried to free herself. Soon the young raccoon, exhausted by its ordeal, sat down and began to cry. Malachi and B'rats crept closer and closer.

"Can we be of any assistance?" Malachi asked the raccoon.

Startled by Malachi's voice, the little raccoon jumped and tried to run away.

"Stop, Stop," shouted B'rats. "We're not going to hurt you. We're going to help you."

With tears in her eyes, the little raccoon agreed to let Malachi and B'rats free it from the can and bottle.

"How in the world did you get into such a mess?" asked B'rats.

"Mamma brought my brothers and me to the river to go fishing," the raccoon explained. "When we got here, we found all this trash. Mamma kept telling us to keep our paws out of the cans and to hunt for frogs and minnows, but I didn't listen."

The little raccoon looked helplessly at its paws.

"First, I found this can with a bean in it, and I just had to feel it. At the same time, this bottle had a shiny piece of foil in it, and I just had to have it, too," it sighed.

"Now I can't get my paws out. I didn't want Mamma to know I'd disobeyed her. When she was ready to go back to the farm, I stayed here and tried to get out of this mess. Now Mamma's gone, and I'm scared and stuck. Please help me," cried the little raccoon.'

"Okay," said Malachi. "B'rats, you work on freeing this paw, and I'll work on the other."

Malachi tenderly but forcefully pushed in on the lid of the can.

"Don't pull your paw out until the lid is out of the way," he said. "It's sharp and could cut you."

"One, two, three—Pull," shouted Malachi as he pushed the lid to the back of the can.

"Oh, thank you, thank you, thank you," shouted the masked little critter. "Now if the other paw will just come out of this bottle, I can go find Mamma."

"B'rats, how are you doing with the other paw?" asked Malachi.

"Not very well," muttered B'rats as he walked around the bottle scratching his head.

Malachi walked over to inspect the situation, and he noticed the raccoon held a little piece of shiny foil in its paw.

"If you'll drop that piece of foil, I think your paw will easily come out of the bottle," suggested Malachi.

"I was just going to suggest that," smirked B'rats.

"Okay," said the excited raccoon.

Sure enough, when the raccoon let go of the foil, its paw easily slid out of the bottle. It was free at last.

"My name is Malachi, and this is B'rats. What is your name?"

"'Ras-calley Raccoon is what my mother named me, but my friends call me 'Miss Calley'."

At that moment, Miss Calley broke into a wailing fit. Large tears rolled down her masked face as she rolled B'rats' long thinly furred tail between her leathery little paws.

"What's wrong, Miss Calley?" inquired Malachi.

"I miss my mamma," blubbered the hysterical raccoon. "She left me here and doesn't know where I am. I want my mamma."

"Well, I want my tail back," snapped B'rats as he snatched it out of Miss Calley's paws.

"We will help you find your mamma," consoled Malachi. "Which way is the farm?"

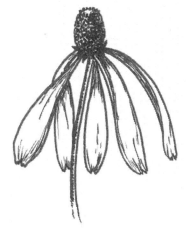

"We'll just follow this trail through the cypress and chinquapin trees by the crawfish pond to the top of the hill. From there we'll see a large **meadow**[24] with beautiful flowers," explained Miss Calley. "Across the meadow is a big barn, a farmhouse, and a big oak tree. My home is in the big oak tree."

Malachi and B'rats bounded off on a new adventure with Miss Calley leading the way. Along the way, they jumped honeysuckle vines and

---

[24] **Meadow** – A treeless field or flat area of land covered with grasses and wildflowers. *Example: The butterflies flew throughout the meadow in search of flowers.*

bounced over limbs and ferns. Miss Calley's long waddling strides left B'rats and Malachi behind. Luckily, like all curious raccoons, Miss Calley loved to investigate, feel, and touch everything. While she poked and prodded in each knothole and under every rock, Malachi and B'rats had a chance to catch up.

"I don't like this," whispered B'rats. "That raccoon is going to get us into trouble."

"What makes you think that?" asked Malachi

"Just look at her. She has her paws on everything; those frisky fingers never stop. She's always feeling things, including my tail. Did you see how she felt my tail like it was a stick or something? I just don't like it. She wouldn't be in this mess if she'd just kept her paws out of that can and bottle."

Miss Calley started digging in the ground as B'rats complained.

"Just—just look at her," he added. "She's found a hole in the ground, and she can't keep her paws out of it. This situation is not good."

As B'rats and Malachi finally caught up with the bouncing ring-tailed fur-ball, they noticed muddy, red clay now covering her fur. Miss Calley was digging vigorously into perfectly round holes in the ground.

"What in the world are you doing, Miss Calley?" inquired Malachi.

"Digging for **crawfish**[25]," answered the mud-covered coon. "Crawfish are the best-tasting food in the world."

"Well, I'm starving," B'rats said. "And I love fish. The last fish dinner I had was behind Fipple's Fish Market. I just can't wait. How do you catch these fish?"

"Well, all you have to do is dig around in these holes, and you'll catch one," replied Miss Calley.

B'rats found a hole with mud balls stacked neatly around it.

"Is this a crawfish hole?" asked B'rats.

"Sure is," replied Miss Calley. "I'll show you how to–"

[25] **Crawfish** - Animals that live in fresh water and look like little lobsters. A crawfish is called by different names in different areas of the United States: crawdad, mudbugs, and crayfish are all common. *Example: The crawfish protect themselves with their large front claws and their ability to swim backwards very quickly.*

Before Miss Calley could finish her sentence, B'rats stuck his nose into the hole he found. He was not to be disappointed.

Suddenly, B'rats let loose a horrid, gruesome scream. He found his dinner—attached to his whiskers.

The terrified rat squeaked at the top of voice, leaping into the air with one upset crawfish attached to his whiskers.

"Help me. Help me," cried B'rats, but Miss Calley and Malachi could only laugh. Soon the crawfish released B'rats and crawled back into its hole, never to be bothered by a hungry rat again.

Chuckling, Miss Calley bounded up the trail and left Malachi to soothe B'rats' injured feelings.

"I told you. Did I not tell you?" B'rats griped. "This coon is nothing but a bouncing fur-ball of trouble." He stroked his sore whiskers.

"She didn't tell you to poke your **snout**[26] into that hole," said Malachi, chuckling. "She said fish, and your monstrous appetite took control of your ratty, little brain. You're the one who stuck his nose in a hole in the ground— not Miss Calley."

Malachi left B'rats and continued up the trail after Miss Calley. As he ambled along, he heard B'rats behind him mumbling something about his tail and whiskers.

Before long, the sky became brighter, and the three adventurers could see a large clearing in front of them. It was the meadow—a beautiful, large meadow filled with fragrant wildflowers and green grass.

Miss Calley looked at B'rats.

"Are you still hungry?"

B'rats immediately grabbed his whiskers and nodded his head, yes.

"Over on the other side of the split-rail fence and down the trail there's a peach **orchard**[27]. If we are very careful, we can slip over there without the dog catching us. Okay, let's go," whispered Miss Calley.

---

[26] **Snout** -A long projecting nose. *Example: The dog had long whiskers on its snout.*

[27] **Orchard** – A group of nut or fruit trees that have been planted as an agricultural crop. *Example: The peaches were ripe and ready to pick in the orchard.*

With Miss Calley in the lead and Malachi and B'rats running behind, the three made their way across the meadow. As they approached the orchard, the aroma of fresh peaches was just about all the starving rat could endure. In a matter of seconds, Miss Calley and Malachi fell behind as B'rats led the way.

"Would you look at the size of these peaches?" exclaimed Malachi, peering into a tree.

"And just how are we going to get them off that tree?" snapped B'rats.

"You just stand back and watch," said Miss Calley.

She scampered up the trunk of a peach tree loaded with big, beautiful, juicy peaches. Miss Calley knocked out a peach, and it dropped on D'rat's tail with a thud. The rat was so hungry, he didn't even notice.

After eating their fill of peaches, the three travelers decided to rest. Miss Calley found a comfortable fork in the top of the peach tree, and Malachi and B'rats curled up in the warm sunshine at the tree's base and fell into a deep sleep.

NOTES

Chapter Five
Danger in the Barn

As honeybees buzzed from flower-to-flower gathering **pollen**[28], Malachi, B'rats, and Miss Calley snoozed in the afternoon sun. Soon, a gentle breeze carried a familiar stench, catching the attention of the sleeping trio.

B'rats batted his sleepy eyelids and nudged Malachi.

"What is that disgusting odor?"

Malachi responded by snuggling deeper under the large sycamore leaf he used as a blanket. The sleepy little mouse said nothing. He just yawned, stretched, and went back to sleep.

At that moment, a shiny black nose and two glistening eyes peered around the trunk of the peach tree. B'rats did not move.

"Malachi," he whispered.

Malachi rubbed his sleepy eyes and looked into the terrified face of his friend.

"What's wrong, B'rats?" asked Malachi. "And what is that foul odor?"

The speechless rat could only stare at the shiny, black eyes looking back at him. Recognizing his friend's fear, Malachi slowly turned around.

"It's a little Pooey," shouted Malachi.

"A Pooey?" Miss Calley questioned from the top of the tree. "What

---

[28] **Pollen** – A fine powder produced by the flower of a plant. *Example: Bees and other insects carry pollen from one plant to another.*

in the world is a little Pooey?"

Miss Calley scurried down the tree trunk.

"You boys don't know anything," she laughed. "This is a skunk. And I might add, this little Pooey, as you call her, is one of many. Just look at the little critters running around in their striped coats."

"The little stink-pots are everywhere," growled B'rats as he held his nose.

"How dare you refer to my **kits**[29] as stink-pots?" snapped the irritated and defensive mother.

"Look, B'rats. It's Pooey U. Stink," said Malachi. "I'm sorry, we did not recognize you."

"Oh, that's quite all right," said the radiant skunk as she batted her long eyelashes and whisked her luxuriant tail from side to side.

"Are these your little stink-pots?" asked B'rats

"I'm not a little stink-pot," remarked a boastful little skunk. "My name is Musty, and— and this is my brother Stinky D, and— and we can run faster and jump higher than any old rat."

"And you smell worse, too," shouted B'rats as he watched the little skunks bound into the meadow chasing butterflies.

"Where are you going on this warm beautiful day?" asked the friendly skunk.

"We're going to find my mother," Miss Calley said. "Have you seen her anywhere?"

"I saw your mother last night on the trail leading from the river," the skunk responded. "She mentioned that she was taking your brothers to the corn patch for supper. I cautioned her to be careful because Ras-PU-ton, the hound dog, was

[29] **Kits** – A family group of young or baby animals of certain animals. *Example: A baby skunk is called a kit, and several baby skunks are called kits.*

busy patrolling the garden area. That was the last time I saw her. Have you checked in the den tree behind the farm house?"

"Not yet, but we are on our way to the den tree now," said Miss Calley.

Off bounded Malachi, B'rats, and Miss Calley across the orchard toward the farmhouse. As they crossed beneath the peach trees, Miss Calley vaulted the tall sage grass that had overgrown the once groomed orchard. It was all Malachi and B'rats could do to keep up with the agile raccoon.

When Miss Calley came to the **split rail**[30] fence, she slowly crouched and scanned the barnyard for Ras-PU-ton. The out-of-breath rodents soon joined Miss Calley at the fence.

"Can we rest for a minute?" begged B'rats.

"Only for a minute. This isn't a safe place to rest," whispered Miss Calley. "That old hound dog is always sneaking up on me. Nothing pleases that **canine**[31] more than to chase me up a tree."

While B'rats and Malachi rested under the shade of a dandelion plant, Miss Calley kept her keen senses alert for any sign of Ras-PU-ton.

All of a sudden, out of the tall sage grass, a large animal lunged toward Miss Calley, scaring her so badly she leaped to the top of the split rail fence. Malachi and B'rats crouched under the grass and hid. It was Ras--PU--ton. Malachi and B'rats shuddered and held on to each other as the large hound growled and barked at their terrified friend.

With her ears laid back and bristles up, Miss Calley defended herself as well as she could while perched high on the top rail of the rickety fence.

Suddenly, Pooey bounded out of the tall grass, wheeled around and took aim at the attacking hound. With her tail raised high and with the force of an atomic bomb, Pooey sent a yellow cloud of **musk**[32]

---

[30] **Split rail** – A fence rail split from a log. *Example: The long wooden rails were perfectly stacked to make a beautiful split-rail fence.*

[31] **Canine** - A species of mammal. Dogs, fox, coyote, and wolves are all mammals.*Example: A canines can be a domestic or wild animal.*

[32] **Musk** - an oily liquid with a strong odor. *Example: The skunk sprayed musk from its scent gland.*

toward the snout of the barking dog.

The two rodents couldn't believe their eyes. Ras-PU-ton had been "odorized" by Pooey. The only thing the helpless dog could do was whine, yip, roll, and tumble in the grass. With his nose on the ground and his front legs crumpled beneath him, the humiliated hound used his hind legs to propel himself across the meadow as if he were plowing a **furrow**[33] with his nose, trying to rid himself of Pooey's undesirable perfume.

"Oh, thank you, Pooey," said a relieved Miss Calley. "I don't know what we would have done if you hadn't come along."

"Yeah, you were terrific," added Malachi.

"Well, it will be a while before that hound bothers you again," said Pooey. "I don't think that dog will ever learn."

"Pooey, have you sprayed the hound before?" asked Malachi.

---

[33] **Furrow**- a trench or indention in the soil. *Example: The farmer plowed a furrow then planted and covered the corn seeds.*

"Of course. Why do you think we call him Ras-PU-ton? He smells more like a skunk than he does a dog. I odorize him every chance I get," said the delighted skunk.

With a proud bounce, Pooey pranced her way back to the center of the meadow where she joined her kits for a late afternoon nap.

Miss Calley, B'rats, and Malachi continued their way through the grass at the edge of the barnyard. Once they arrived near the barn, Miss Calley gave Malachi and B'rats instructions.

"See the barn over there," said Miss Calley as she pointed. "I think we need to stay in there until it gets dark and then make our way to my home in the **snag**[34]."

Malachi and B'rats both nodded in agreement.

"Follow me," whispered Miss Calley. She led the way with Malachi and B'rats close behind.

They passed the pigpen, the chicken yard, and finally the horse corral. As they approached the barn door, Miss Calley stopped and listened very carefully.

"Be very careful in the barn," she cautioned. "Some....things in the barn might be dangerous to little rodents like you."

Malachi and B'rats' eyes grew large, and B'rats immediately grabbed his tail and began twisting it.

"What do you mean dangerous?" B'rats timidly asked.

"Well, just stay with me, and I don't think you will be eaten," said Miss Calley.

"I'm not going in there," protested B'rats.

"What is in the barn that might eat us?" asked Malachi.

"Fritz and Henry keep watch on the **corn crib**[35]," said Miss Calley. "They're always on the lookout for Eeede."

"Who in the world is a Fritz and Henry, and what is an Eeede?" asked B'rats.

---

[34] **Snag** – a standing dead tree. *Example: The hollow snag had many holes in the trunk and made a perfect home for squirrels.*

---

[35] **Corn Crib** – A place in a barn where corn to feed the animals is stored. *Example: The corn is picked and stored in the corncrib so the farmer could feed his animals throughout the winter.*

"**Reptiles**[36]," answered Miss Calley. "Fritz and Henry are King snakes, and they rule over the barn. And Eeede is a mean, black rat snake that eats eggs and—

Oh, never mind."

"S-s-sn-snakes? Did you hear what Calley said, Malachi?" shouted B'rats. "There is only one thing worse than a cat, and that is a snake. Malachi, if we go into that barn, we are as good as dinner for some scaly reptile."

"I have to agree with B'rats," said Malachi. "Cats are bad, but snakes are nightmares for little rodents like us."

"Oh, don't be silly, I'll be with you all the time," Miss Calley reassured them. "Don't worry. Just come on, and we'll find a safe place for you in the hay loft, close to Owlfred. He will protect you."

"Who-who-who is Owlfred?" asked B'rats.

"He's a good friend of mine," said Miss Calley.

"Let me rephrase that question. WHAT is Owlfred?" asked B'rats.

"He's a **barn owl**[37]," said Miss Calley.

"That does it," shouted B'rats. "I'm going back home. Alley cats will be a welcome sight. This whole refuge idea is one continuous nightmare. First, I was dumped into a garbage truck, thrown onto a garbage barge, and stuffed into an opossum's pouch. After almost drowning in a raging river, I had to crawl into a log with an arrogant, smelly skunk. I have been attacked by a crawfish and a dog. Now you are telling me that there is a good chance I will end up as

---

[36] **Reptiles** – Animals that cannot produce their own body heat and have dry scaly skin. *Example: There are many different kinds of reptiles in the world, including snakes, lizards, turtles, alligators and crocodiles.*

[37] **Barn owl** – A large owl with a soft heart shaped face. *Example: The graceful Barn owl flew out of the top of the barn in search of mice in the meadow.*

46

an owl pellet or a tasty reptile dinner? My whiskers have been pulled on and almost out, and my nerves have worn all the hair off my tail. I look a mess. I'm going home to those wonderful, temperamental, predictable, alley cats."

"And just how are you going to get back home?" asked Malachi. "You couldn't find your way out of a peanut shell, let alone back to the city. Let's listen to Miss Calley. She'll take care of us."

"Are you two through complaining?" asked Miss Calley. "Owlfred is a good friend of mine, and he has a score to settle with Eeede. I know he won't bother you. Now follow me to the loft."

As Miss Calley, B'rats, and Malachi slipped through a crack in the boards of the ragged old barn, the smell of fresh hay and sweet feed filled the air. Dusty beams of sunlight pierced through the dimly lit barn. Hundreds of dusty spider webs decorated the massive wooden beams holding the barn together.

Malachi and B'rats looked around the barn and realized just how small they were when compared to their surroundings. They saw a playground of fun and food—sacks of grain and a full corncrib just waiting to be plundered. For just a moment, B'rats forgot about Fritz, Henry, and Eeede and focused his attention on all of the food around him.

"We have found it," shouted B'rats.

"Shhhhhh," hissed Miss Calley.

"Malachi, we're here. We've found the refuge," exclaimed B'rats.

Malachi grabbed his friend by the whiskers and tried to quiet him.

"What in the world are you doing, B'rats?" whispered Malachi. "Shouting like that is ringing the dinner bell for those reptiles. Now hush."

B'rats smacked Malachi on the paw.

"What did I tell you about my whiskers?" he asked angrily.

"Both of you be quiet," scolded Miss Calley as she climbed across the sacks of grain to a ladder leading to the loft. "Now follow me, and keep up. Don't be lagging behind."

With Miss Calley leading the way, B'rats and Malachi followed step after step until they made it to the loft.

Miss Calley carefully scanned the area and assured her two nervous friends the snakes were not there.

"We will stay up here until dark then we can cross the open yard to see if Mamma is in the den tree," said Miss Calley.

"When do we eat? I'm starving," said B'rats. "Did you see all that corn down there, Malachi? It's like a pot of gold at the end of a rainbow."

"You'll just have to wait, B'rats," said Miss Calley. "When Owlfred wakes up, we'll have him stand guard while we eat."

"Where is Owlfred?" questioned B'rats.

"Oh, he's not far," giggled Miss Calley.

"Well, what does he look like?" the nosey rat inquired.

"Oh, he looks just like that tower of feathers you're leaning against," snickered the raccoon.

At that instant, the large pillar of feathers B'rats had been leaning against moved. B'rats fainted dead away. Little did he know he'd made himself comfortable next to Owlfred.

The beautiful, large **raptor**[38] gracefully turned his head and slowly opened his large, sleepy eyes. The exquisite, heart-shaped face of the barn owl left Malachi speechless. Amused and tickled by the entire ordeal, Miss Calley continued her busy work as she felt in every crevice and corner of the loft.

"Good afternoon, Calley," said Owlfred in a deep rich voice. "Did you bring my lunch today?"

"Hello Owlfred," chuckled Miss Calley. "How are you doing today?"

"Well I would be doing fine if I weren't so hungry," said Owlfred, winking at the raccoon.

"These are my friends, B'rats and Malachi. B'rats is the one passed out," she snickered.

"He's just playing possum," whimpered Malachi in a trembling voice.

"No, Malachi, I think he's really fainted this time," said Miss Cal-

---

[38] **Raptor** – A family of large birds that have sharp, hooked bills and long claws called talons. Raptors hunt and eat birds, small mammals, reptiles, fish, and large insects. *Example: Hawks, eagles, owls and falcons are all raptors.*

ley before turning to Owlfred.

"B'rats and Malachi saved my life," she said. "I had my paws stuck in a can and a bottle, and they rescued me."

"That doesn't surprise me, Calley. You never will learn to keep your paws out of places they don't belong," said the astute owl.

"Tell me about it," said B'rats, who by now had started to regain his senses. "You would not believe the trouble that raccoon can get into. Let me tell you about this coon...."

"Hush, B'rats. Let Calley talk before—" whispered Malachi.

"I promised B'rats and Malachi you wouldn't eat them because you're my friend," stated Miss Calley. "Do I have your word that you won't eat them, Owlfred?"

"I don't know, Calley. That fat rat looks like he'd make an awfully good owl pellet," said the cagey owl, loudly popping his bill.

Once again, B'rats fainted, and Malachi jumped into a stack of hay.

"Oh, he's only joking," laughed the raccoon.

Malachi slowly nudged his head out of the haystack, and B'rats wiggled his tail and opened his eyes. The large owl chuckled and offered B'rats a suggestion.

"In order to escape from a snake, it is wiser to run away than to play possum."

With those few words of wisdom, the majestic owl ruffled his feathers, popped his bill, closed his eyes, and fell asleep.

Malachi grabbed B'rats' tail and pulled him into the stack of hay. They both curled up and went to sleep with Miss Calley and Owlfred nearby.

NOTES

Chapter Six
Predator Parade

As the sun sank in the west, squeaking sounds in the rafters of the barn awakened Malachi and B'rats. Strange bird-like creatures flew out of a small door in the top of the old building.

"Those are the ugliest birds I've ever seen," whispered B'rats.

"I know, Malichi answered. "Just look at the poor creatures. They have fur instead of beautiful feathers and sharp little teeth instead of a beak. Would you look at the ears on that one? I've never seen a bird with ears."

"What kind of birds hang upside down when they sleep?" asked B'rats.

Owlfred slowly ruffled his feathers and opened his large, dark eyes.

"You silly rodents. Those aren't birds. They're **bats**[40]. Bats are mammals just like you. They roost in the top of the barn until it's dark and then they fly out over the meadow and catch insects to eat."

"Do they eat rodents?" asked B'rats in a quivering, timid voice.

"No," responded Owlfred, "but that does remind me, I'm getting awfully hungry. I think I'll go to the meadow and find a **shrew**[41] for dinner."

[40] **Bat**- Very small nocturnal mammals that eat insects, pollen, or fruit. *Example: The little brown bat caught insects while flying over the meadow.*

[41] **Shrew** – A small mouse-like animal with a long, flexible, pointed snout and very small eyes and ears. *Example: The shrew scurried under the leaves of the oak tree searching for earthworms and snails to eat.*

With a large leap, the big white and tan owl flew out of the barn toward the meadow. Malachi and B'rats scurried over to the loft door and peeked out to observe a sight they had never seen.

The sun was sinking behind the distant mountains, and fireflies danced through the misty blanket of moisture hanging over the meadow. The sounds of tree frogs and field crickets singing a melody of courtship tunes made the evening come alive in the meadow. Malachi and B'rats found the sights and sounds of the countryside much more pleasant than the bustling evenings they remembered back in the city. The beauty humbled both of them.

The giant yellow glowing moon rising in the east was a bright spotlight casting shadows on the creatures of the night. In a large snag at the edge of the meadow, Malachi and B'rats saw the silhouette of Owlfred watching for an early evening meal.

"Look, B'rats. There's Owlfred," said Malachi.

"I sure hope he finds plenty to eat. I don't want him coming back hungry," said B'rats.

"Speaking of hungry," Malachi answered, "I could sure use a few kernels of corn."

"Where is Miss Calley? She promised us food," said B'rats.

"I'm over here," answered the sleepy raccoon. "I'm getting hungry, too."

Miss Calley scurried down the ladder with Malachi and B'rats close behind.

"Now stay close to me," instructed Miss Calley as she bounded over a bale of hay. "We'll eat in the corncrib."

Malachi and B'rats climbed over the side of the corncrib and slid into the metal bin.

"Would you look here?" exclaimed B'rats as he smacked his lips.

"This is just like falling into a big pot of gold," remarked Malachi.

"Eat your fill, and be quick about it," ordered Miss Calley. "I want to go to the snag to see if Mamma is there. I miss her so much, and I know she is worried sick about me."

"Quick, B'rats, Miss Calley is in a hurry, and I want to get out of this barn as soon as possible," Malachi said. " I don't want to run into those snakes."

"Don't worry about Fritz," Miss Calley said. "I saw him leave the barn headed for the chicken yard a while ago, and Henry is in the back of the barn. You're safe for a little while. Let's go find Mamma."

"But, but, I haven't finished eating," fussed B'rats.

"We'll go to the **watering trough**[42], and you can get a drink," said Miss Calley. "With all that corn you just put away, you'll swell up like a balloon. You won't be hungry for a long time."

The three companions dashed out the barn door past the pig pen and over to the chicken house.

"Listen," whispered Miss Calley. "Something is in the chicken coop besides chickens. "

Miss Calley, B'rats, and Malachi dashed to the hen house to see why the chickens were squawking. They jumped up to the wire-covered window and peeked inside. Feathers flew and chickens bounced off the walls.

B'rats grabbed his tail, and Malachi grabbed B'rats.

---

[42] **Watering trough** – A large container that is used by farmers to water animals. *Example; The watering trough was filled to the top so the animals could easily drink.*

"What is it, Miss Calley?" asked B'rats.

"It's Eeede, and he's stealing eggs again," said Miss Calley. "Oh, I wish Owlfred were here. He'd put a stop to this."

"Last spring," Miss Calley explained, "Owlfred and his mate, Minerva, built a beautiful nest in the loft of the barn. Minerva had laid three eggs in it. One night while Owlfred and Minerva hunted, Eeede destroyed the nest and ate the eggs—swallowed them whole. Ever since, Owlfred has vowed to get even. He even promised Fritz and Henry they could reign over the barn if one of them could kill Eeede."

"Let's get out of here before Eeede sees us and swallows us whole," whispered B'rats.

"Wait. I see something moving in the corner," said Miss Calley. "It's Fritz, and he's sneaking up on Eeede."

Like a lightning strike, Fritz attacked Eeede. Twisting around each other, the two snakes prepared to fight until only one was left alive. Coiling and **constricting**[43], Fritz wrapped himself around the egg eating reptile, suffocating Eeede. Finally, Eeede's body fell limp.

"Now you know why they call Fritz a King snake," remarked Miss Calley. "He's the king of all snakes. Even the poisonous snakes are afraid of the kings. Now are you two ready to go to the snag? Malachi?? B'rats?? Where are you two?"

The entire ordeal scared B'rats so badly he'd fainted again, this time falling from the window ledge.

"We're down here, Miss Calley. B'rats is playing possum again," answered Malachi.

"Did you faint, too?" asked Miss Calley.

"No, I didn't play possum," said Malachi. "In all of the confusion, B'rats grabbed my tail instead of his own. When he fainted, he jerked me off the window ledge with him."

Miss Calley jumped from the ledge, landing next to B'rats.

"Wake up, you silly rat," said Miss Calley. "This place is safer for rats, mice, frogs, and birds now that there's one less snake around.

---

[43] **Constricting** – To tightly squeeze something. *Example: The King snake wrapped itself around the rat snake, constricting it, until it could not breathe.*

Now let's put that horrible incident out of our minds and go find my Mamma."

The three friends ambled over the woodpile and passed the clothesline. As they scrambled by the farmhouse, they smelled Ras-PU-tin, who was digging in the garbage bin.

Soon they came to a large dead oak tree behind the farmhouse. Miss Calley and her family lived in a hole at the top of the tree. With excitement in her eyes and a spring in her step, Miss Calley bounded up the tree anticipating her mother greeting her at the door.

Unfortunately, Miss Calley was disappointed. Her mother and brothers weren't home and hadn't been there for some time.

B'rats and Malachi waited anxiously at the base of the tree for word from above. Only large teardrops fell to the ground as Miss Calley sobbed.

"Where is my Mamma?" she cried. "I want my Mamma!"

Suddenly a beautiful, graceful bird flew up and landed next to Miss Calley. It was Owlfred.

Don't cry, Calley. You're going to be all right," he said. "Minerva told me last night that your mother and brothers were in the corn patch

eating the farmer's corn. They made the farmer very angry, so he placed traps in the garden and caught your family. Early this morning, he took them to a place south of here. I think it was a place called 'the refuge'."

"Were they hurt?" asked Miss Calley.

"No, they were all fine," said the sympathetic old owl.

"Miss Calley. Miss Calley," shouted Malachi from the bottom of the tree. "We are going to the refuge, and you can go with us."

57

"How will we know which way to go?" sniffed the sad little raccoon.

"Follow the trail across the pasture and down the hill to the beaver pond," directed Owlfred. "When you come to the beaver dam, cross it, and turn left. Then follow the creek until it runs to the **clear cut**[44]. The refuge is on the other side of the clear cut. You can't miss it. There are tall, beautiful trees and clear, clean water in the refuge. You won't have any problems finding your Mamma. Malachi and B'rats will help you."

Owlfred spread his wings and silently flew away.

"We'll leave first thing in the morning," said B'rats.

"Okay," agreed Miss Calley as she made her way down the tree.

"Malachi," whispered B'rats, "I'm awfully thirsty. All that corn I ate needs some water."

"I'm thirsty, too," said Miss Calley. "If we are very quiet, we can slip over to Ras-PU-ton's dog house and drink his water."

"Aren't you afraid he'll wake up and chase you?" whispered B'rats.

"No, that old hound is deaf and sleepy," said Miss Calley. The only thing he can smell right now is Pooey's perfume. My brothers and I used to see how close we could get to Ras-PU-ton before he woke up. Watch, I'll show you."

Miss Calley slipped behind the doghouse and peeked around the corner. Ras-PU-ton was nowhere to be found.

"That's strange," said Miss Calley. "Ras-Pu-ton isn't here, and his food and water haven't been touched. That old hound never misses a meal. Something must be wrong. Keep your eyes open. You never know when he'll show up."

---

[44] **Clear cut** – an area where every tree has been cut and removed. *Example: There are many different timber harvesting practices. One type of harvesting is to clear cut the timber and plant new trees back.*

NOTES

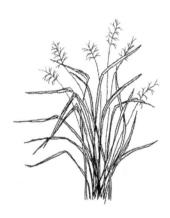

Chapter Seven
A Real Jug Head

As he drank his fill from Ras-PU-ton's water bowl, Malachi heard the muffled sound of an animal whining and whimpering.

"What's that?" he asked.

"I don't know. It sounds like it's coming from the garbage can," said Miss Calley.

The trio slipped around the corner of the house to the trash can.

"Would you look at that?" fussed Miss Calley. "That silly old dog has turned over the can full of trash and made a mess. I'm sure I'll get the blame.

"Look at him. That nosey old dog has his head stuck in a plastic jug, and he can't get it out," chuckled B'rats.

Malachi and Miss Calley raced around B'rats to get a better view of the dog with a jug on his head.

"That's what you call a real JUG HEAD," B'rats added with a smirk.

"Well, we've got to get that off his head," said Malachi.

"Why?" asked Miss Calley. "That's the best that dog has ever looked."

"He'll die if we don't get it off. He can't eat or drink, and he's not breathing well, either," said Malachi. "It's our duty to save him. You have to help, Miss Calley."

"Oh, all right, but he has to promise not to bite me, growl at me, or aggravate me in any way," responded the bright-eyed coon.

Malachi and B'rats quietly slipped over to Ras-PU-ton as he aimlessly stumbled and wandered. Malachi took charge of the situation.

"Ras-PU-ton, my name is Malachi, and this is B'rats," he said. "We'd like to help you get out of that jug."

Apparently, the old dog couldn't hear a word Malachi said and continued stumbling about, bumping into the fence post and barn door.

B'rats suddenly ran up to the hound's head and pounded on the jug. The noise echoed through the plastic jug like a big bass drum, startling Ras-PU-ton so badly he took off running straight toward the farmhouse's screened-in porch.

"Stop him, Miss Calley," shouted Malachi.

Miss Calley leaped on the back of Ras-PU-ton, scaring the disoriented hound even more. Malachi and B'rats had never seen anything like it—an overgrown, jug-headed hound with a raccoon perched on his back and hanging on for dear life.

Once again, B'rats got confused and grabbed another animal's tail. Only this time, instead of Malachi's, he grabbed Ras-PU-ton's. His mistake led to the ride of a lifetime. B'rats clung to Ras-PU-tin's long hairy tail as the crazed dog whisked him around like a knot at the end of a whip.

The trip ended for Miss Calley and B'rats at the wooden steps of the back porch. Ras-PU-ton, blinded with the jug on his head, ran smack into the bottom step of the porch, sending Miss Calley and B'rats sailing into the farmer's petunia patch.

Malachi raced to Miss Calley and B'rats, huffing for breath when he arrived.

"Wh-Wha-What in the world were you two thinking?" screamed Malachi. "If we wanted to kill the dog, we would have let him suffocate. Now he's probably had a heart attack."

"You told me to stop him, and that was the only idea that came to mind," Miss Calley said. "Besides, I've always wanted to do that."

Malachi just shook his head and looked at B'rats.

"B'rats, did you actually think you were going to stop him by pulling on his tail?"

"Nope, just grabbed the wrong tail again," the embarrassed rat said with a shrug.

"Is he dead?" asked Miss Calley as she eased over to the limp dog.

"Good grief!" shouted Malachi. "I don't know. He's still breathing, but if we don't remove this jug, he won't be for long. He needs oxygen, or he'll die. Pull on the jug, Miss Calley, and see if it will slip off his head."

"I'll probably live to regret this," mumbled Miss Calley.

"Uhhh... Uhh...," moaned Miss Calley as she tugged at the jug. "It won't budge."

"Just bite his tail," said B'rats. "Tail-biting got me out of a bottle once."

"I'm not going to bite that nasty dog's tail," shouted Miss Calley. "If you want to bite it, be my guest."

"Nope; not in a million years. The dog is going to die," said B'rats.

"Well B'rats, we're just going to have to chew through the jug so Ras-PU-ton can breathe," said Malachi.

"Okay," B'rats agreed. "I'll start on this side. You get on the other side."

As B'rats and Malachi began the rescue operation, Miss Calley explored the old hound's features. Fascinated by the large paws on the canine, she couldn't resist tickling and feeling the leathery, rough pads on the bottoms of his feet. The long bony, tail that Ras-PU-tin dragged behind him seemed a pathetic excuse for a tail compared to the beautiful, lush ringtail Miss Calley proudly possessed.

Malachi and B'rats soon chewed two large holes through the tough plastic holding the four-legged mammal hostage.

"He can breathe now," said Malachi. "B'rats and I are going to have to chew this thing off his head."

Malachi looked at Miss Calley.

"I need you to watch Ras-PU-ton through these holes. Tell us if he wakes up."

"Okay," said the enthusiastic coon as she moved from Ras-PU-ton's tail to his head.

As Malachi and B'rats began gnawing through the top of the jug, Miss Calley's curiosity got the best of her. She poked her busy paws through the holes of the jug to feel Ras-PU-ton's ears, nose, and eyes. It was the most fascinating adventure she had ever had.

A loud pop signaled that Malachi and B'rats had successfully completed their task. The jug slipped off Ras-PU-ton's head, and the hound was free at last.

"Why won't he wake up, Malachi?" asked B'rats.

"He has a nasty bump on his head from his encounter with the porch step. He'll come around in a few minutes."

"Let me help," said a voice from the window ledge of the screened in porch.

"Who are you?" asked Malachi as he looked up.

"My name is Stubby."

Malachi and B'rats looked at Miss Calley and asked, "What's a Stubby?""Stubby is a **chipmunk**[45]. He lives in that hole over there by the petunia patch," said Miss Calley.

"Well, what can Stubby do that we can't do?" B'rats asked boastfully.

---

[45] **Chipmunk** – A small ground squirrel with cheek pouches and a flat hairy tail. *Example: A chipmunk carries acorns and seeds in its cheek pouches to store in its underground burrow.*

"Just a minute, and I'll show you," said the little chipmunk. "I'll be right back."

The speedy, little chipmunk dashed over the rocks in the flower-bed and around the corner toward the birdbath.

In the meantime, Miss Calley pinched, poked, and prodded the old dog, as she tried to wake him up. She grabbed Ras-PU-ton's whiskers and felt around his mouth. A naturally nosey creature, Miss Calley had to find out what was under the sagging, drooling lips of the hound dog. Very carefully, she lifted the top lip and revealed his glistening white teeth–large teeth. Stunned by her discovery, Miss Calley gasped and looked at Malachi.

"Did you know these were in here?" whispered the astonished coon, pointing to the large canine teeth of the hound.

"Leave that poor old dog alone," snapped Malachi.

"Yeah," B'rats agreed, "You're going to feel him to death."

At that moment, the souped-up ground squirrel, complete with racing stripes, sped back around the corner. Stubby carried enough water cached in his pouches to extinguish a small forest fire, and he ran right up to Ras-PU-ton's snout. With a mighty blow, Stubby sprayed water all over the old hound's face. Slowly, Ras-PU-ton's eyelids began to open.

Not knowing what to expect next, Malachi, B'rats, and Stubby ran behind Miss Calley, who was now looking into the hound's eyes. It was evident Ras-PU-ton was confused and in pain. Without making a sound, he slowly stood on his wobbly legs and stumbled to his dog-house. He stayed there for the rest of the evening.

"Poor Ras-PU-ton," said Stubby. "That pitiful dog doesn't even know what happened to him. He probably thinks Miss Calley whipped him."

"Stubby, you did a great job," said Malachi. "Let me introduce myself. My name is Malachi, and this is my friend B'rats."

"Pleased to make your acquaintance," said the polite, little rodent.

"We're on our way to the refuge to find a new home and help Miss Calley find her family," said Malachi.

"Well, before you leave, would you like something to eat?" asked Stubby.

"Food?" smacked B'rats as he licked his lips. "Real, honest to goodness rodent food?"

"Well, I wouldn't eat anything else," said Stubby. "I'll be right back."

Like a streak of lighting, Stubby raced to a bird feeder where sunflower seeds covered the ground. As B'rats peeped around the corner of the porch, he could see Stubby stuffing seeds into his mouth.

"Look at that, Malachi," said B'rats. "How is Stubby doing that?"

"Doing what?" asked Malachi.

"Where is he putting all of those seeds?" asked B'rats.

"Here he comes. Be quiet, and don't embarrass me by asking stupid questions," said Malachi.

Zipping over rocks and around flowers, Stubby looked like a gasoline-powered miniature pack mule carrying a cargo of sunflower seeds. The speeding fur-ball skid to a stop right in front of B'rats.

"P-pooooo...." sounded from Stubby's mouth as he unloaded his cargo of sunflower seeds.

"How did you do that?" asked B'rats.

"Do what?" Stubby asked.

"How did you carry all those seeds in your mouth?"

"I have cheek pouches. You know, little, built-in grocery carts," said Stubby.

He wheeled and sped off for another mouthful of seeds.

"Did you hear that, Malachi? He has pouches. I wonder where he got them. Do you realize all the food I could eat if I had pouches?" asked B'rats.

"You silly rat. Stubby was born with pouches," said Miss Calley as she devoured the sunflower seeds.

Soon Stubby was back with another mouthful of seeds.

"Well, it's past my bedtime, so I will see you in the morning," said Stubby as he headed to his home in the petunia patch.

B'rats watched carefully as Stubby scurried through the entrance to his underground home. Soon the diligent, little chipmunk began pushing dirt from the inside of his **burrow**[46], safely sealing the en-

---

[46] **Burrow** – A hole dug in the ground by an animal. *Example: The chipmunk made himself a safe home by tunneling a burrow under the rocks.*

trance of his home and securing it from any predator that might want to make a meal of Stubby during the night.

"It's been a long day," said Miss Calley, yawning. "I think I'll go to sleep in the oak tree one more time before we go to the refuge. You and Malachi can sleep in the petunia patch tonight. I'll wake you in the morning, and we'll go to the refuge to find Mamma."

NOTES

Chapter Eight
Birdfeeder Air Attack

As the early morning sun rose over the towering treetops, Malachi and B'rats awoke to a strange thumping noise. Malachi looked out of his makeshift home to see Stubby attached to a large, red apple. Both Stubby and the apple bounced down the porch stairs. Ker-thump, Ker-thump, Ker-thump.

Malachi couldn't tell if Stubby was moving the apple, or if the apple was moving Stubby. After reaching the bottom of the stairs, Stubby began rolling the apple to his burrow.

"Good morning, Stubby," said Malachi.

"Good morning," replied Stubby. "I suppose you'll be leaving for the refuge this morning?"

B'rats popped his head from beneath a large, yellow petunia.

"An apple," shouted B'rats. "Where did you get that?"

"On the screened-in porch," said Stubby. "The farmer's wife just brought out a basket of big juicy red ones. Crawl up the steps, and get one. They're delicious. Don't let the farmer's wife catch you, or you could end up like me—tailless."

"And that's why they call you Stubby?" asked Malachi.

"Yep. One day I was helping myself to a basket of nuts on the back porch when the farmer's wife came out. She didn't like nut thieves. When she grabbed her broom, I quickly ran for the door. Just as I was about to make a hasty exit, she grabbed the door and slammed it. Needless to say, not all of me made it out of the door."

"Oh...." gasped B'rats, grabbing his bony tail.

"It's better now," Stubby continued. "I think the lady feels sorry for me. She always leaves nuts and fruit on the porch for me now. She actually seems to like me, but I don't think she's too fond of rats. You'd better be careful."

"I'm not that hungry after all," grumbled B'rats. "Where did you get the sunflower seeds you brought us last night?"

"Over there, under the bird feeder. Go around the corner and over to the **birdbath**[47]. The farmer just put out some corn and sunflower seed this morning," Stubby said "I have to get this apple chewed up and put into my burrow. If I don't see you again, have a safe trip to the refuge."

"Okay," shouted Malachi and B'rats as they rounded the corner to find something to eat.

"Would you look at that?" whispered B'rats. "There are sunflower seeds, corn, and fruit. It's like a picnic dinner waiting for someone to

[47] **Birdbath** – a shallow bowl or container that holds water for birds for bathing. *Example: Colorful birds were lined up on the edge of the birdbath.*

come along and enjoy it."

"Look at the beautiful birds," exclaimed Malachi.

Brightly colored yellow and black goldfinches decorated the small bushes around the birdbath. Red cardinals sang from the evergreen and dogwood trees bordering the yard. A pair of doves strutted and pecked as they ambled around the yard searching for sand and **grit**[48]to fill their **crops**[49].

"This has to be a safe place to eat," whispered B'rats. "Just look at all of these birds. They won't mind sharing their food with us."

As Malachi and B'rats began munching on the corn and grapes, the birds became very quiet and still. Many flew away, disappearing into the tall bushes and trees.

"Malachi, where did everybody go, and why is it so quiet around here?" whispered B'rats.

"I don't know," said Malachi. "Grab a grape, and let's hide behind these rocks."

Like a bolt of lightning, something swooped through the feeding area. It passed so quickly that B'rats and Malachi almost missed seeing it, but they sure heard it and felt a gust of wind.

"What was that?" asked B'rats.

Before Malachi could answer, the large bird zoomed through the yard again, only this time carried its prey.

B'rats and Malachi could only look at each other as tiny feathers floated to the ground.

"Malachi, I think it's time to leave," said the nervous rat.

"I believe you're right," said Malachi. They raced back around the house.

When they turned the corner, they didn't realize Stubby headed toward his burrow with another large apple.

CRASH! BOOM!

Rodents and apple parts flew everywhere. Malachi and B'rats

---

[48] **Grit** – Fine sand or pebbles. *Example: Certain birds will eat grit to help grind up food in their digestive track.*

[49] **Crop** – A crop is an expandable pouch in the throat of birds. *Example: The bird ate until it filled its crop.*

landed in the petunia patch, and Stubby and his apple rolled over and over, finally coming to rest at the foot of the old oak tree.

"Why in the world are you two in such a hurry?" shouted the angry chipmunk.

"Didn't you see it?" shouted B'rats.

"See what?" asked Stubby.

"That bird. That big bird that grabbed the little bird."

"Oh, I forgot to tell you about the falcon," said Stubby.

"You forgot....YOU FORGOT," B'rats shouted angrily as he paced and rubbed his backside. "I mean, why would anyone remember to tell us something like that?"

"Now, B'rats," said the diplomatic Malachi. "Stubby probably thought you knew all about the falcons."

"And just where would I have learned about falcons?" snapped B'rats.

"Everybody knows about falcons," said Stubby. "They are just as dangerous as cats."

"Well, ex-cuse me for being so stupid," snapped B'rats. "I have no idea what a falcon is, but I am listening if you would like to tell me, Mister Chipmunk."

"That falcon was an American Kestrel," Stubby explained. "He eats insects and small birds.... and sometimes rats. He has large claws called talons, a sharp hooked bill, and his eyesight is so good he can see rats hiding behind rocks while he flies high in the sky."

"I've heard enough. Cats on the ground... falcons in the air," shouted B'rats. "It's time to leave for the refuge. I need to relax before I have a nervous breakdown."

"Thanks, Stubby," shouted Malachi as he and B'rats headed toward the meadow where Miss Calley was enjoying the sunshine and foraging for berries and insects.

As the three friends romped and bounced through the meadow,

excitement and anticipation filled them, along with a bit of fear. They had no idea what to expect once they entered the forest.

Slowly, one at a time, they slipped into the dimly sunlit pine and hardwood forest. Miss Calley took one last look at her home and knew she probably would never return to the farmhouse and the old oak tree. She'd always remember Owlfred, Pooey, and Stubby, not to mention the fun-filled hours that she spent teasing old Ras-PU-ton.

A large lump swelled in Miss Calley's throat as she followed Malachi and B'rats into the woods.

NOTES

Chapter Nine
Lily Pad Bounce

As the three woodland travelers entered the tall majestic forest, new sights, smells, and sounds filled the air to alert their curious senses. Large ferns danced in the breeze and brilliantly colored birds flew from tree to tree. A new adventure surely loomed around every turn in the trail as they made their way to the refuge.

A loud noise from above Miss Calley suddenly frightened her, and she forgot all about missing her old home.

"Jaaay, Jaaay," shrieked a bird from the overhanging limb of a hickory tree.

"Are you folks traveling or looking for food?" asked a large **blue jay**[50].

"We—we're going to the refuge," said the startled Miss Calley.

"Who are you?" asked B'rats as he peeped from behind a fallen limb.

"My name is Slick, and this is my brother, Douglas," said the handsome blue and white bird.

"Do you know how to get to the refuge?" asked Malachi.

"Sure do," said Douglas as he knocked a hickory nut out of the top of the tree.

"Well, can you tell us which way to go?" asked B'rats.

[50] **Blue jay** – A medium-sized bright blue and white bird with a crest of feathers on the top of its head *Example: The blue jay aggravated the gray squirrel by pulling at his tail.*

"Sure can." said Douglas, knocking another hickory nut from the tree.

"How long will it take us to get there?" asked Miss Calley.

"A while." replied the mischievous blue jay as he dropped still another hickory nut.

"This bird is getting on my nerves, and he's going to hurt someone with those nuts," snarled B'rats.

"Oh, if he wanted to hit you, he would have done it by now," boasted Slick. "Douglas is the best bombardier in the woods. Nothing on the ground is safe when he's airborne."

"Well, he's dropping them awfully close to my tail. My tail and I don't need any more aggravation," said the disgusted rat.

"Please help us get to the refuge," pleaded Miss Calley.

"Okay," said Slick. "Just follow me, and I'll take you to the **beaver**[51] pond. The Paddlewackers can tell you how to get to the refuge from there."

"Who and what is a paddlewacker?" whispered B'rats.

"I guess we'll soon find out," said Malachi.

The trio began chasing the brilliant blue and white birds.

As Slick flew from branch to branch, Malachi, B'rats, and Miss Calley bounded over logs and dodged low-hanging limbs, hustling to keep up with the ever-chattering bird. Douglas brought up the rear of the caravan, aggravating B'rats by dropping pinecones, branches, and acorns from the tops of the trees.

"How far to the beaver

[51] **Beaver**- a large semiaquatic broad-tailed rodent that is native to North America. *Example: The beaver swam across the pond, climbed on the shoreline, and pulled a large tree branch into the water to carry to its lodge.*

pond?" asked B'rats in a tired, grumbling voice.

"Just down the hill," said Slick. "Be very careful when you get to the bottom. Sly lives down here, and he's always looking for a meal."

B'rats came to a screeching halt.

"Malachi," he shouted

"I know, B'rats," whispered Malachi. "Just grab your tail, and come on."

"Answer me one question, Malachi," sighed B'rats. "Is there a FREE FOOD sign hanging off my back? I'm tired of being at the bottom of the **food chain**[52]. I want to be a lion, a tiger, or a bear and chase everything instead of being chased."

"I don't know, B'rats, but if we wait around here, I'm afraid we will find out. Come on," said Malachi.

"No," said the tired and crabby rat.

"Just what do you mean no?" asked Malachi.

"I mean no. I'm just sick of running," said B'rats. "No matter what this Sly is, I'm going to give him a piece of my mind."

"Well, that shouldn't take up much time," mocked Douglas.

"Look, B'rats, I've come too far for you to end up as dinner for anything. Now come on before I jerk a knot in your tail," snapped Malachi.

All of a sudden, from the top of the tree, the two jays began squawking loudly. Slick and Douglas had spotted Sly crouching next to a large downed tree.

"Jay, Jay, Jay!" screamed Douglas and Slick. "Run for your lives!"

Miss Calley raced down the hill toward the beaver pond, scampering up the first large cypress tree she found.

Sly pounced from behind the log, landing directly in front of the two rodents. Malachi and B'rats were trapped nose-to-nose with Sly, a beautiful **red fox**[53].

---

[52] **Food Chain**- The arrangement of plants and animals according to food sources. *Example: One example of a food chain is: insects eat microorganisms; a small fish eats insects; a large fish eats a small fish; and an eagle eats a large fish.*

[53] **Red Fox** – A small reddish-brown dog-like mammal with a large, bushy, white-tipped tail. *Example: A fox captures its prey by being very quick and smart.*

"Bombs away," shouted Douglas as he dropped a large hickory nut.

The nut landed on top of Sly's head with a loud Ker-plunk, dazing the hungry fox.

"Direct hit!" announced Slick as he flew a low swoop over Sly's head. "Run, you crazy rodents, before he regains his senses."

As Malachi and B'rats escaped down the hill, they heard the sounds of more hickory nuts bouncing off Sly's head and back. After each Ker-plunk, Slick shouted, "Direct Hit."

At the bottom of the hill, Malachi and B'rats came to a large body of water.

"The beaver pond," shouted Malachi, tumbling head over tail to the water's edge.

"Don't stop, Malachi," shouted Miss Calley from the top of the cypress tree. "Sly is right behind you!"

While Sly raced down the trail toward Malachi and B'rats, Slick tormented the fox by swooping down and plucking fur from his tail. Douglas continued bombing Sly with pinecones, dead branches, acorns, and anything he could use to slow the fox down.

Malachi and B'rats faced a dilemma—water in front of them and a hungry fox coming quickly from behind.

A large bullfrog at the water's edge startled the two hysterical rodents as it jumped onto a **lily pad**[54] floating on the water.

"Look," shouted Malachi, pointing to the frog.

The frog jumped onto another large leaf.

"Follow me," said Malachi.

Malachi and B'rats jumped from one large leaf to another and another until they were out of Sly's reach.

Disgusted, angry, and hungry, Sly paced at the water's edge while Slick and Douglas chattered with excitement from the top of the cypress tree. The fox was defeated and began wandering his way around the pond looking for an easy meal that didn't involve jaybirds and rodents.

"Okay. What now, Malachi?" asked B'rats, clenching the large lily pad leaf.

"Let's head to that island," said Malachi, pointing to a mound of mud and sticks in the pond. "It looks safe there."

Malachi and B'rats again bounced from lily pad to lily pad across the pond. Before long, the 'lily pad bounce' became a new game for the two rodents. Bouncing and hopping on the leathery, green leaves decorated with bright yellow and white flowers made them forget about all of their troubles—at least for a minute.

From Miss Calley's high perch in the tree, she saw Malachi and B'rats playing in the pond. She also saw a bullfrog swimming to the bank. The hungry coon thought about how good that frog would taste if she could manage her way down the tree and to the edge of the pond without being seen.

Miss Calley slowly climbed down the large, shaggy-barked cypress tree. Without making a sound, she tiptoed around the tree's base and crouched, waiting for the chance to catch the green and brown **amphibian**[55].

Little did Miss Calley know that slipping around the other side of

[54] **Lily pad**- a large, round floating leaf of an aquatic plant. *Example: The lily pads' bright white flowers were beautiful floating on the ponds surface.*

[55] **Amphibian** -An animal that lives the first stage of its life in the water, then lives as on land as an adult (frogs, toads, and salamanders). *Example: The large frog, an amphibian, jumped in the water to escape danger.*

the tree was another animal waiting to catch its own easy meal.

Focused on the frog, Miss Calley's muscles were taut; she was ready to pounce. Just as she lunged for the frog, she caught a glimpse of a large gray and black animal leaping from the other side of the tree. As Miss Calley soared through the air, she knew she'd reached the point of no return. All she could do was land and hope she and the other animal didn't collide.

Ker-splash. Coon tails and coon feet splashed everywhere. Miss Calley was drowning the most handsome coon in the woods.

Ears laid back, snorting, growling, and flinging mud, sticks, and wet leaves into the air with her front feet, Miss Calley let the frog thief know he was the reason her dinner was swimming away.

"Pardon me," said a handsome male raccoon. "I had no idea such a fine-looking lady was around. Please forgive my manners,"

The apologizing raccoon fished in the water in search of a peace offering.

"You scared me," fussed Miss Calley. "Worse than that, the best tasting meal of the day is swimming away."

"I am truly sorry. Please forgive me. Let me introduce myself. My name is Ruckus," said the coon as he bowed. "And what might your name be?"

"Miss Calley," muttered the embarrassed little coon.

"You sure are a beautiful raccoon," said Ruckus, teasingly.

"Oh, P-lease," shouted B'rats from a lily pad. "I believe I'm getting ill. Malachi, is she actually gonna fall for that gibberish?"

"I think it's kind of nice," said Malachi.

"Well, if you will excuse me," said Miss Calley, "I must join my friends. Maybe I will see you again."

"Oh, you can count on it," said Ruckus with a soft growl.

With stars in her eyes and love in her heart, Miss Calley bounded onto one of the closest lily pads. Both coon and lily pad sank straight to the bottom of the pond.

B'rats laughed so hard he rolled off his lily pad and into the water. Seeing Miss Calley leaping and sinking lily pads was just more than he could handle after watching Ruckus trying to sweep her off her paws.

As the wet rat swam and Malachi bounced across the pond, Slick and Douglas landed on a fragrant, butterfly-covered button bush that grew atop the mud and stick island. Before long, a wet and flustered Miss Calley Coon joined them.

NOTES

Chapter Ten
Meet the Paddlewackers

The three water logged travelers finally arrived at the island in the middle of the beaver pond, soaked, cold, and hungry but glad to be alive. As Malachi, B'rats, and Miss Calley dried themselves, Douglas and Slick got excited. They all heard a strange noise behind the island.

"What is that hissing sound?" whispered Malachi.

"Oh no," shouted Miss Calley. She bounded off the island and back into the water, swimming for her life as the hissing became louder and louder.

Douglas and Slick immediately took to the air and shouted alarms. Malachi and B'rats wheeled around to face two large, gray, flapping wings and a head attached to a very long neck.

"Sssssssss," hissed the provoked bird.

Malachi began burrowing a hole in the mud. Poor B'rats grabbed his tail and ran in circles.

Malachi soon disappeared beneath the logs, dried mud, and decaying leaves.

"Help, help, help!" shouted B'rats as the large, white and gray goose peered at him over a log.

"Sssss-stay away from my babies," hissed the aggressive goose.

With that, the goose turned and waded into the water on the other side of the small island. The frightened rat couldn't believe what he saw. The hissing and honking bird floated on the water, and seven little, yellow, paddling powder-puffs floated behind her.

"Whew," sighed B'rats, wiping his brow. He then began looking for Malachi.

"Malachi.... Mal-a-chi," shouted B'rats as he peered down the hole into which his friend had escaped. "Where are you, Malachi?"

While B'rats searched for his friend, he heard something swimming in the water behind him. Miss Calley was coming back to the island. When B'rats turned around to greet her, his tail slipped into the hole Malachi had created.

All of a sudden, something grabbed B'rats' tail and jerked him down the hole.

"Yee-oow,," shouted B'rats as he fell into a dimly lit, wet room.

"Malachi," B'rats said angrily. "What have I told you about pulling my tail? I have told you time and time again that no rat looks good with a bob tail."

The irritated rat reached over to smack Malachi, but he became confused. He could feel Malachi's soft fur, but there was a lot more of it....a whole lot more.

"Malachi, you sure have gained weight," whispered B'rats as he continued to feel around the dark room. "Malachi, what large feet you have."

B'rats reached up to feel the rodent's face, and he discovered giant teeth.

"Oh my," shouted B'rats. "We've got trouble. Big trouble, big, big, big trouble. Ma-la-chiiiii!"

"It's all right, B'rats," a familiar voice said from the other side of the large room.

"What have you gotten me into now?" asked the nervous rat.

From above, Miss Calley heard Malachi and the frantic rat. She began digging her way through the sticks and wet vegetation to rescue her friends.

"I'll save you," shouted the little coon.

As she removed the logs and mud from the top of the island, beams of sunlight illuminated the inside of a beaver lodge and its occupant, a very large, flat-tailed, web-footed, brown rodent with giant orange teeth.

"Oh my. Oh my, my," gasped B'rats.

"I take it you are a beaver," said Malachi.

"That is correct," nodded the distinguished looking creature.

"Colonel Forest Woodrow Paddlewacker is the name, and **gnawing**[52] logs is my game," he chuckled.

"Well, allow me to introduce myself. I'm Malachi and this is my friend, B'rats."

While the introductions took place, Miss Calley slipped her busy little paws through the top of the beaver house. Her fingers began investigating the furry head of Colonel Paddlewacker. Miss Calley poked her fingers in the dignified Colonel's ears, eyes, and nose. Puzzled by her unusual behavior, when the Colonel opened his mouth to protest, the silly coon put her fingers into his mouth.

"Phooooooo," sputtered the beaver.

Miss Calley jerked her paws back and peered through the hole, eyeball-to-eyeball with an animal and the biggest set of choppers she had ever seen. She looked at her paws, making sure they were still attached to her legs.

[52] **Gnawing** – Chewing on wood, bone or other hard surfaces. *Example: A rodent's teeth constantly grow so they must gnaw on wood to keep their teeth trimmed and sharp.*

"Whss-shoooooo," she sighed after quickly counting her fingers.

"Excuse me, but have you seen my friends, Malachi and B'rats?" asked Miss Calley.

"We're down here," said Malachi.

"And we're coming out," shouted the nervous, tail-twisting B'rats.

"You'll have to excuse B'rats, Colonel Paddlewacker," Malachi said. "He's had a very tense day. Between blue jay bombings, a hungry fox, and the recent goose attack, B'rats and his tail have had about all the stress they can handle."

"And if you will excuse me, I need to see some sunlight," added B'rats. He climbed his way back to the top of the **beaver lodge**[53].

"I must go, also," said Malachi. "We'll repair the damage we caused to the roof of your house."

"Don't worry about it. Those kits of mine need to learn how to repair a hole in the roof," said the large, brown, teardrop-shaped animal.

"Where is your family?" asked Malachi.

About that time, a small head popped through an entrance in the floor of the beaver lodge, and a little beaver crawled out of the water onto the neat, chip-covered floor. Two more followed, with a large beaver bringing up the rear.

Shy and timid, the three little kits huddled close to their mother and watched Malachi.

"Hello, my name is Malachi. What are your names?"

"This is my mate, Fanny Mae Paddlewacker, and these are our three kits, Fidget, Furfit, and Fret Paddlewacker," said the proud Colonel.

"Come on, Malachi," shouted B'rats from the roof. "I'm hungry and tired."

"Well, I must be on my way," said Malachi.

"You are welcome to stay the night on the roof and eat

[53] **Beaver Lodge – The home of a beaver. Example: The beaver family constructed a lodge mad**e *of mud, sticks and vegetation in the middle of the pond.*

cattails with us," said Fanny Mae.

"Thank you for the invitation. We would be glad to," said Malachi.

Malachi wiggled his way through the roof of the beaver house, and found B'rats and Miss Calley playing in the water at the edge of the beaver lodge.

"I like it here," said Miss Calley as she pawed in the water and flipped minnows onto the roof of the beaver lodge. "Since you're so hungry, eat one of these minnows, B'rats. They are really good."

"No thanks. I'd have to be pretty hungry to eat a fish again. Boy, how I'd just love an old hot dog on a moldy bun. There's nothing out here but berries, insects, and those blasted hickory nuts," said B'rats as he rubbed a knot on his head.

"Good news. Good news," shouted Malachi. "The Paddlewackers have invited us to spend the night on the roof and eat with them."

Expectations quickly filled B'rats' mind.

I'm a rodent, and the Paddlewackers are rodents—large rodents.

Naturally, they'd have access to large quantities of rodent food like potato chips, cookies, cake, hot dogs, and popcorn. B'rats could already taste them.

"Yes, yes, yessss," shouted the starving, drooling rat. "What are we eating?"

"**Cattails**[54]," said Malachi.

"Cat tails?" shouted B'rats.

"Who in their right mind would eat the furry tail of a cat?" he gasped. "This is just great. First, I have a nervous breakdown, and now you expect me to starve to death. I have had it. Just write me off as a dead rat."

B'rats snatched a minnow away from Miss Calley.

"This is as low as a rat can get," he mumbled.

The minnow slipped out of his paws and swam away.

"MMMmmmmmmm," B'rats sighed.

A commotion on the other side of the beaver pond caught the attention of the three hungry travelers. It was Ruckus chasing the

---

[54] **Cattail** - A tall wetland plant with furry spikes *Example: The cattails growing around the pond was a perfect place for dragonflies to rest.*

mother goose and her **goslings**[55]. Ruckus prowled for an easy gosling meal, but he was having a difficult time separating the goose from her goslings. Mother goose finally chased the wet and humiliated Ruckus up a tree, gathered her babies, and paddled to the center of the lake.

"Oh great," said B'rats. "Just when things are bad, they get worse. That honking mass of feathers is headed our way."

"Well, I'm leaving," announced Miss Calley. "I want no part of that goose."

She gently slipped into the water and swam to the shore where Ruckus climbed down from the willow tree that had saved him from a goose flogging.

In the meantime, Malachi and B'rats became concerned about the threat of being goose whipped themselves. Suddenly, Colonel Woodrow and Fannie Mae Paddlewacker surfaced from their underwater habitat, followed by their three little Paddlewackers—Furfit, Fidget and Fret.

"You need not concern yourself with the goose," the Colonel said. "She won't hurt you. She only worries about raccoons, foxes, and coyotes."

"Sometimes a **bobcat**[56] will wander by," added Fannie Mae. "She gets real concerned about them. Other than that, she's a great neighbor."

"Did you say bobcat?" asked B'rats.

"Yes," nodded the Colonel.

"I have heard of alley cats and calico cats, but I have never heard of a cat named Bob. What or who is a bobcat?"

"A bobcat is a large, dangerous cat with a short stubby tail," said the knowledgeable beaver.

"So then...I take it this is where we get cattails for supper," said B'rats. "If so, I am not yanking the tail off a juiced-up woods-cat. I

---

[55] **Goslings** – baby or young geese *Example: Mother goose chased the predator away from her goslings.*

[56] **Bobcat** – A bobcat is about twice the size of a house cat. It has a short, stubby tail and long tuffs of hair on each cheek. *Example: A bobcat can jump high and run fast when pursuing its prey.*

don't care how hungry I get."

"No, no, no," chuckled the Colonel. "A cattail is a plant. Beavers don't eat animals. We are herbivores. We only eat plants and tree bark."

"But you are rodents, and rodents eat hot dogs and cookies and rotten food," insisted B'rats.

"You must be a city rodent. Country rodents eat grain, and nuts—healthy foods," said Fanny Mae.

B'rats looked at Malachi.

"Figures, they are a bunch of health nuts," he whispered. "We are going to starve."

Fanny Mae, Fret, Furfit, and Fidget slid into the water, returning with a mouthful of cattails. They offered the mass of wet roots and stems to Malachi and B'rats. Reluctantly the two accepted the muddy vegetation. Fidget, Furfit, and Fret began munching the long potato-like roots.

"Yummmm, Yummmmm!"

The Colonel smacked as he ate.

"Try them, you'll like them," he said.

Malachi took a little nibble out of the root.

"Well, what do you think?" asked Fannie Mae.

"Not bad at all," said Malachi as he munched some more. "Try it, B'rats."

B'rats took a bite out of the large root.

"Well, I guess it will do if nothing else is available," said the rude, grouchy rat. "

"Just what does a beaver do all night?" asked Malachi.

"We are very busy," explained the Colonel. "When we wake up late in the evening, the first thing we do is clean our house."

"That figures," mumbled B'rats. "Healthy and neat. The kind of animals that give rodents a bad name."

"Hush," whispered Malachi.

"Then we patrol the dams to make sure all of the water is at the correct level. If the dam has a leak, we have to fix it," said Col. Paddle-wacker.

"You work, too?" shouted B'rats.

"Well, of course," said Fannie Mae.

"Are you sure you're rodents?" asked B'rats.

"Certainly. Our teeth constantly grow just like yours. That makes us rodents, too," said Furfit as he meticulously groomed his fur.

"Mama said we have to chew on wood so our teeth will stay sharp and strong," said Fidget.

"If our teeth aren't sharp and strong, we could starve," added Fret.

"All right, kits. It's time for you to start cleaning the lodge," said Fannie Mae.

The three kits jumped into the water and swam about splashing and diving under lily pads. Soon they headed for the underwater entrance to the beaver lodge.

After Malachi and B'rats had eaten their fill of cattail roots, Colonel Paddlewacker invited them to spend the night on the roof of the beaver lodge. The two smaller rodents agreed the roof would be a safe place until morning. They settled down for the evening while the beaver family went about their nightly chores.

As the sun slowly sank behind the large cypress trees, the still pond came alive with new and strange sounds. Malachi and B'rats had tucked themselves in between the leaves and sticks of the beaver house, but they heard the sounds of large bull frogs bellowing and small tree frogs croaking. Schools of minnows scattered in the shallow water's edge as large bass patrolled in search of an easy meal.

The full moon rose in the east, illuminating the mist-covered pond as small, brown bats darted about catching insects. At the edge of the hardwood forest, a family of screech owls sang an eerie song, but Malachi was too impressed with everything else to be afraid.

"Isn't it beautiful here?" he asked no one in particular.

"It's wet, noisy, and everything is hungry," answered B'rats. "Including me. Have you ever noticed that everywhere we go something is trying to eat us? Rats and mice must be food for every animal alive."

"Well, we've been lucky so far," said Malachi. "Now try to go to sleep."

"I wonder if Miss Calley will come over and sleep on the beaver lodge tonight?" asked B'rats.

"I don't think so. She's taken a real interest in Ruckus. Maybe we'll see her in the morning," yawned Malachi. "Good night, B'rats."

"Good night, Malachi." B'rats rolled over and nodded off to sleep.

Life was so pleasant at the pond that B'rats and Malachi delayed their trip to the refuge for several weeks. The two friends spent many fun-filled days and cozy summer nights on the roof of the beaver lodge as guests of the Paddlewackers. Douglas and Slick airlifted acorns, mushrooms, and berries while Fidget, Furfit, and Fret Paddlewacker served as a personal ferry service to and from the shore. Even a refuge couldn't have as many conveniences as the pond did.

NOTES

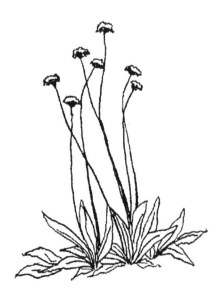

Chapter Eleven
Search and Rescue

The early morning rays of sunlight ushered away the dark shadows of night. Malachi shivered. The air held an unusual chill. The once lush green leaves that had danced gracefully in the gentle summer breeze had been touched by nature's autumn paintbrush. Brilliant red, yellow, and orange leaves desperately clung to the once nourishing limbs while the cool north wind blew. Autumn had arrived, and the hot, steamy days of summer were a memory.

"Burrrr," shivered Malachi as he stretched and yawned in the crisp morning air. To his left, he could see B'rats curled up and still sleeping under a large cottonwood leaf.

As Malachi looked at B'rats sleeping soundly, he noticed a mosquito perched on the tip of D'rat's nose. This annoying little insect was about to tap into breakfast, and B'rats was the buffet. Being as still as a mouse could be, Malachi prepared to smack the bloodthirsty insect.

B'rats opened his eyes and saw the mosquito attached to the end of his nose. He also saw Malachi ready to smack the hungry mosquito.

"Poooo, Poooo, Poooo," B'rats blew upward from his bottom lip in an attempt to frighten the needle-nosed insect, but the cold mosquito was slow to move.

With the force of a mighty mouse muscle, Malachi delivered a blow to D'rat's nose.

"Are you crazy?" shouted B'rats.

"Bug problems?" asked a deep voice from across a small,

beaver-chewed log.

"No, I don't have bug problems. I have slap-happy mouse problems. What business is it of yours anyhow?" snapped B'rats.

"Quite frankly, I suppose it is none of my business," said a large bullfrog. "But I could have saved you a lot of pain if you would have just remained still. I'm a professional bug and insect exterminator—the fastest tongue in the **swamp**[57]"

"Well, aren't we special?" chattered B'rats. "I don't need a bug killer, especially some slick-skinned, flat-footed, quick-tongued, skeeter-eater. And I could care less about your life story, especially when I'm in so much pain."

"Oh, B'rats, you act like I tried to hurt you. Your nose is fine, and you're being extremely rude to—to—, I'm sorry, I didn't get your name," said Malachi as he turned to the large green and brown frog.

"Most everyone calls me Frog, but I like Skeeter-Eater much better. I think it fits me, too," said the large eyed creature with a permanent grin spanning from ear to ear.

"Well, then, Skeeter it is. My name is Malachi, and the whining rat's name is B'rats," chuckled Malachi.

Before B'rats had a chance to fuss at Malachi, a voice from overhead rang across the beaver lodge.

"Incoming!" shouted Slick.

"Take cover," Malachi warned, scrambling to hide under a log.

It was only Douglas delivering breakfast to B'rats and Malachi. Ker-plunk.

"Direct hit!" shouted Douglas as he circled the beaver lodge once and glided in for a landing on the button bush.

"Ouch, ouch, ouuuuccch," shouted B'rats. "That does it. That nut landed right on my head."

"Yes, it did. Getting good, aren't I?" boasted the giddy blue jay. "My, we sure did wake up in a foul mood.

"Where is Malachi?" asked Douglas.

"Here I am. Did you say something about breakfast?" asked the

---

[57] **Swamp** – low-lying ground covered in shallow water: also known as a bog or marsh. *Example: Many unusual plants and animals live in the swamp.*

hungry mouse.

"Sure did. I found an old walnut tree and a pecan tree loaded with nuts. The pecans are sweet and delicious," said Douglas. "Slick is over there right now eating his fill. Would you like me to bring you more?"

"Not until I find a hole to get into," snapped B'rats as he rubbed his head and held his tail.

"Would you like to join us for breakfast?" asked Malachi.

"I don't eat nuts, just insects like mosquitos, mayflies, and dragon flies. In fact, be real still. There's a mosquito on the leaf just over your head," said Skeeter.

Quicker than a blink, the frog zapped his sticky tongue out and caught the tiny insect.

"Wow," shouted Malachi. "We should call you 'Lightning' instead of Skeeter. You do have the fastest tongue in the swamp."

"Delicious, just delicious," said Skeeter, smacking his lips and grinning.

B'rats had eaten the first pecan Douglas had delivered.

"Where is that top-notched bird with the rest of my breakfast?" demanded B'rats. "I'm ready for him this time."

"What's on your head?" asked Malachi.

"A hickory nut shell," said B'rats. "You know—a helmet. That bird is not going to knock another knot on my head."

The clever rat tucked his tail under a log.

Sure enough, Douglas approached at a low altitude, and this time he had reinforcements. Slick also carried two large nuts as cargo.

As they flew across the beaver lodge, the two jays released the pecans and walnuts.

"In coming!" shouted Malachi, diving under the log.

Nuts fell all around B'rats, but he bravely stood in the shower of food.

"You missed," shouted B'rats waving to Douglas in defiance.

Douglas then dropped a very large walnut from his beak.

"Did not."

This walnut was so large that the sight of the incoming nut sent B'rats scrambling for the nearest log. Unfortunately, he could only save his head and body. His precious tail took another direct hit.

"OOOOoooooooh," shouted B'rats as the pain shot up his tail and into his spine.

"I want to go home, Malachi. I'm getting too old for all this," he whined.

"I kind of like it here," said Malachi.

"Oh, this is a wonderful place to live," Skeeter agreed.

"But we have no place to stay and no good food to eat," argued B'rats as he gnawed through the pecan shell to reach the tasty nut inside.

"Well, just what kind of habitat does a rat need to survive?" asked Skeeter.

"A habitat without jay birds," groaned B'rats, attending his sore tail.

"Now, B'rats," said Malachi. "Everything we need is here—food, water, and I'm sure we could find shelter. And there is more space than we could ever use."

"Well, as you can see, there is plenty of water thanks to Colonel Forest Woodrow Paddlewacker and his family," said Skeeter. "If not for them, this would be a small dry creek in the hot summer months. The goose wouldn't have a place to raise her goslings, Ruckus wouldn't have a place to fish, and I couldn't live in a dry forest."

"Speaking of raccoons, where is Miss Calley?" asked Malachi.

"She's swimming out here right now," said Slick as he landed in the cattails growing next to the large button bush.

"Well, when she gets here, we'll need to decide whether to go on to the refuge or stay at the pond," said Malachi.

"I've found the best place for you to live," squawked Slick.

"I have too," said Miss Calley as she pulled her soaked body from the pond. "It's just perfect. A hollow sweet gum tree next to the pecan tree. There is plenty of food, it's near the water, and there is room for everyone."

"A real coon-dominium with lake-frontage," snickered Douglas.

"I'm not living with a coon, especially a wet one," announced B'rats.

At that moment, Miss Calley shook her coat and drenched B'rats.

"Well, Miss Calley, would you live with a wet rat?" asked Douglas as he mischievously raised and lowered the crest on his head.

"I've had about all the lip from blue jays I can tolerate," shouted B'rats. He began chasing Douglas around the beaver lodge.

"That settles it," said Malachi. "B'rats needs a home."

"I'll take you to the tree where we will live," said the excited little raccoon. She jumped into the water and began swimming for shore.

"There goes the neighborhood," said Skeeter peeking out from under a large leaf. "This pond is home to two too many raccoons, and they like to eat frog legs for lunch."

Skeeter jumped into the water and headed for the large lily pad.

"Come on, B'rats," shouted Malachi. "Let's go see our new home Miss Calley has found."

As Miss Calley led the way, Malachi and B'rats bounded from one lily pad to another until they reached the bank. Slick and Douglas flew from limb to limb and watched the little caravan making its way around the pond to a giant tree. Limbs, heavy and drooping with rich tasty pecans, signaled that food was abundant for many animals living in the area.

"MMMmmmmmm. groceries," mumbled B'rats as he passed under the nut-producing tree.

Next to the pecan tree stood an old sweet gum tree that towered above all the other trees around the pond. The giant hollow trunk of the old tree had many openings and cavities that offered homes to animals. A small opening at the base of the tree led to the center of the hollowed-out animal apartment complex.

"Look, B'rats," said Miss Calley. "You and Malachi can live here." She pointed to the tiny opening.

"I will live up there in that hole just below Ruckus," she said.

"Just what I always wanted. A lakefront coon-dominium next to a nut store," said B'rats as he pointed to the pecan tree.

Malachi ambled over, sniffed around, and poked his head into the small opening.

"This is perfect," said Malachi. "We'll move in right now."

"You move—I'm going for lunch," said B'rats as he scurried to the pecan tree.

B'rats began searching in the leaves and vines under the pecan tree for delicious nuts. When he had two armfuls, a nut fell from the tree and bounced off the rodent's head.

B'rats threw down his pecans and began shouting.

"This has gone far enough. Bird, there is no room left on my head for another knot. You have done it now," shouted the angry rat.

As B'rats looked up searching for Douglas, he saw only a large mass of leaves and sticks in the entangled vines.

"Come out of there, you stupid bird," he shouted.

B'rats grabbed the vine and began pulling and yanking.

"Come out of there now, and fight like a real bird," he said.

As B'rats scanned the tree limbs looking for the mischievous blue jay, he spied a large red squirrel at the top of the pecan tree enjoying the tasty nuts and discarding the empty shells. Embarrassed and aggravated, B'rats began picking up the nuts he had so childishly thrown to the ground. Suddenly came an alarm from the top of the tree.

"Bark, bark, bark!" chattered the squirrel before he scurried to the backside of the tree. The squirrel's alarm concerned B'rats. He had heard humans walking and talking as they came closer to the beaver pond.

Hiding behind the large roots of the pecan tree, B'rats saw the humans. There were two men, and they wore large boots and carried a box with a wire dangling down its side. The men paced back and forth along the shore talking about all the water the beaver dam held in the pond.

B'rats quietly and carefully slipped back to his new home to alert Malachi about what he had heard. Slick and Douglas were already aware of the presence of the two strangers.

"Malachi, Malachi, Come quickly," urged B'rats.

"What is it?" asked Malachi.

"Look at those two men on the shore over there. They are talking about the Paddlewackers and all the water."

Malachi looked up and saw Douglas and Slick perched on a limb overhead.

"Douglas and Slick, fly over and listen to what the two men are saying."

"The Paddlewackers might be in danger," said Malachi.

After the two birds flew to investigate, Malachi and B'rats paced while awaiting their return. Douglas was first to arrive.

Flying at the speed of light, Douglas dived in and offered B'rats and Malachi his report.

"You are right, Malachi," he said. "They're going to blow up the beaver dam. We've got to do something, and it has to be done quickly," warned the breathless bird.

"Here's what we'll do," said Malachi. "Douglas, you and Slick find Skeeter and tell him to inform the Paddlewackers. Hurry. This is a matter of life and death for all of us. The Colonel will know what to do."

"Okay," whispered Douglas. Malachi watched as the bird flew to the center of the pond where Skeeter sunned himself on a lily pad beside the beaver lodge. He then turned to B'rats.

"You go find Miss Calley. We may need her help," said Malachi.

Douglas told Skeeter of what was about to take place. Without hesitating, Skeeter dived into the water and swam through the underwater entrance of the Paddlewacker's home.

"Colonel Paddlewacker, wake up," croaked Skeeter, popping his head into the beaver house. "Please wake up now. It's a matter of life and death!"

The Colonel and Fanny Mae, startled by the frog's arrival, jumped to their feet.

"What's the problem, Skeeter?"

"It's the men again. They are back with THE BOX, and you know what that means."

The news disturbed the Colonel and his family. They quickly abandoned the beaver lodge, following Skeeter. The frog and beavers swam underwater away from the dam until they reached the other side of the pond. When they surfaced, they could see the two men approaching the dam with THE BOX.

"What are they doing?" asked Douglas from his overhead perch.

"They are going to destroy the biggest dam I have ever built," the Colonel answered with a long sigh.

Skeeter then spoke up.

"What's worse is that if Malachi and B'rats are on the other side of the dam, they'll be washed away when the men blow it up."

"We've got to warn them," said Douglas.

As Douglas flew to save B'rats and Malachi, the men poked and prodded the dam with tools. Douglas kept circling overhead, but he saw no sign of his two friends. Slick sat high in the old sweet gum tree scolding the men, but his effort was useless. The men paid no attention to the screeching bird.

Douglas could not spot Malachi, B'rats, and Miss Calley. Helpless, the Paddlewackers, Skeeter, and the two blue jays could only hope their friends were safely away from the dam and not downstream.

Suddenly, a giant explosion erupted at the base of the beaver dam. Mud, sticks, leaves, and water flew a hundred feet into the sky. The blast ripped a hole in the dam, and a small ocean roared down the old creek bed, spilling over its banks, and flooding and washing away everything in its path.

Proud of their accomplishment, the two men gathered their tools and headed back up the trail leading back to the farm.

As soon as the commotion ended, the Paddlewackers and Skeeter jumped into the water and swam to the broken dam.

"Did you find Malachi and B'rats?" asked Fret.

"No," shouted Slick. "I can't find Miss Calley, either. They can't be in their home because it's under water. I hope they're safe."

As the water continued pouring through the hole in the dam, the gap grew wider. Douglas heard a small voice downstream faintly shouting for help.

"Listen," shouted Douglas.

"Help, help," cried the voice.

"Look, it's Miss Calley, and she's stranded on an old snag hanging over the raging water," said Slick.

"Let's go," said the Colonel. He floated with the water through the break in the dam followed closely by Fannie Mae, Fidget, Furfit, Fret, and Skeeter. Slick and Douglas soared between the trees to help rescue one of their lost friends.

Just before the Colonel could reach where Miss Calley clung to dead limb, it gave way. Both the limb and raccoon dropped into the raging water.

"Hang on to the log," shouted Colonel Paddlewacker.

"We'll save you," said Fidget.

The three little beavers swam closer to Miss Calley.

The wet and frantic raccoon bobbed in the turbulent water in a desperate attempt to keep her head from going under. Furfit and Fidget finally reached Miss Calley and wedged their bodies on each side of the log. From there, they escorted her downstream toward calm water. Fret followed close behind.

When the beaver kits reached the shore with Miss Calley, the Colonel inquired about their two lost friends.

"Miss Calley, have you seen Malachi and B'rats?"

"Yes, they floated passed me while I hung on that snag. I tried to rescue them, but I couldn't reach."

Upon hearing Miss Calley's report, the Colonel ordered a tactical search and rescue mission.

"Douglas and Slick, you search for Malachi and B'rats from the air. Miss Calley, you comb the water's edge, and the rest of us will search in the water," commanded the Colonel.

As the rescue team took to air, land, and water, the rushing current carried the animals many miles downstream. The evening sun began to sink in the west, and the rescuers grew tired and hungry. Still, they found no sign of Malachi and B'rats.

After abandoning their search for the evening, the jays began to look for food in the thick forest. Colonel Paddlewacker and his family foraged on the tender vegetation along the stream bank, and Skeeter croaked and gobbled down insects as they flew passed.

Miss Calley, exhausted, crawled up into the fork of a tree and fell asleep without eating supper.

NOTES

Chapter Twelve
An Old Flat Board

The sun peeking through the trees signaled the arrival of another morning. Miss Calley opened her eyes to a strange new forest. She could think only of her friends and wonder if they were still alive. She missed Malachi and B'rats, but most of all she missed Ruckus, her raccoon friend.

Slick and Douglas, who had spent the night perched in the top of the tree above Miss Calley stretched and fluttered their wings. Douglas noticed a movement in the leaves under the tree. It appeared to be a large raccoon.

"Ruckus," shouted Douglas. "What are you doing here?"

Upon hearing Douglas, Miss Calley scurried head first down the large cypress tree to see her friend.

"I heard what happened and wanted to make sure you and your friends were all right," said the handsome coon.

"Oh, Ruckus," Miss Calley said. "Malachi and B'rats are lost. Have you seen them?"

"No, but I will help you search for them," he said.

After eating a meal of crawfish and **mussels**[58], the two raccoons and their friends resumed searching for Malachi and B'rats. Colonel Paddlewacker and his family had already been in the water the stream

---

[58] **Mussel** - a type of shellfish that has a long dark hard shell and lives in rivers, streams and lakes. *Example: A raccoon will hunt for mussels along a rivers edge.*

but had had no luck.

As the rescuers moved farther and farther downstream, the waterway grew very wide, and the forest grew dense. The huge hardwood trees towered over the tiny ferns and delicate woodland flowers on the forest floor.

Suddenly Miss Calley caught a glimpse of something small nestled under a large fern. Whatever it was appeared soft, gray, and as still as a-a "mouse!" shouted Miss Calley.

Sure enough, it was Malachi, and not too far away they found B'rats curled up under an old flat board.

Slick swooped down from the sky to confirm Miss Calley's discovery.

"It's true. It's true," shouted Slick, "They are here."

Malachi and B'rats had floated down the river all day and all night. They became so exhausted they hadn't thought of all the fuss their friends might make over them.

"Allow me to wake up B'rats," whispered Douglas. He flew to an oak tree and plucked a large acorn off the limb. With careful aim, Douglas released the large nut dead center on the rat's tail.

"You stupid bird, I'll get you for this," shouted B'rats as he jumped up from a sound sleep.

Startled by all the commotion, Malachi woke up. Before him were all his friends.

"We thought we would never see you again," said the teary eyed little mouse.

"Are you all right?" asked Fannie Mae. "We have been so worried about you. Are you hungry?"

"I'm so hungry my belly fur is tickling my backbone," said B'rats.

"In-coming," shouted Slick.

"Oh no," whimpered B'rats. "I can't believe I really missed those bombardier birds."

After a delicious meal and a little rest and relaxation, the beavers, birds, frog, Malachi, and B'rats discussed the new problems facing them. They had traveled many miles from their home and were far too tired to return. Skeeter and the Paddlewackers, in fact, had no home to return to at all. B'rats and Malachi hadn't even moved into their new home before the dam explosion. Miss Calley was content anywhere, as long as Ruckus was with her.

As the animals pondered their fate, Fidget, Furfit, and Fret explored the stream, pushing mud and gnawing on sticks and roots. Furfit noticed an unusual, flat, brown piece of wood that B'rats had spent the night under. Suddenly a small dragonfly landed right on the middle of the board.

"Psst, Skeeter," whispered Furfit. "Look. What is on this flat board? It's a dragon fly, and I bet you can't catch it."

With a giant leap, and a loud plop, the frog landed in the middle of the flat board but missed the handsome fly.

"Can't get them every time," laughed the frog.

"What are all these markings on this board?" asked Fidget.

"It's writing, like in the newspapers," said B'rats. "What does it say, Malachi?"

"I can't see it. Bring it closer," instructed Malachi.

The two little beavers pushed the board closer to the shore, and Malachi jumped in excitement.

"Oh my. Oh my, my," said the excited mouse. "We are here, B'rats. We made it. This is a sign that was washed away by the water."

"Well, what does it say?" asked Slick.

"It says, 'REFUGE: All plants and animals protected'," announced the delighted little mouse. "This is our new home, B'rats."

As the tired but happy travelers looked about them, they saw towering trees loaded with nuts of all kinds. The bushes and vines drooped heavy with wild fruits and berries, and the ground was rich with delicious mushrooms and insects. The ancient forest provided a variety of shelters for the animals to make home. A gently flowing clear stream meandered through the center of the forest providing moisture to the plants and animals dwelling in the unspoiled natural habitat.

As Malachi, B'rats and their friends stood silently, calm and peaceful expressions spread across their faces.

Colonel Paddlewacker looked at Fanny Mae.

"This would be a good place to build a dam. What do you think?"

"I think if we get started now, we could have a home for Skeeter by morning," said the bubbly mother beaver.

"B'rats, that old log over there with a hole in the side looks like a good place for us," commented Malachi.

"We'll sleep anywhere," screeched Slick and Douglas as they flew up to a low hanging branch. "We'll keep watch while you build your homes."

Miss Calley and Ruckus surveyed the creek bank and found an old hollow tree gently leaning over the stream.

"Miss Calley, I think this would be a good place to raise a family," said Ruckus.

"Oh, Ruckus," giggled Miss Calley.

"Great. Just what the world needs—more coons with busy fingers," mumbled B'rats.

As Malachi, B'rats, Ruckus, and Miss Calley settled into their new homes, Skeeter watched the tireless Paddlewackers construct a dam. By dawn, the beaver dam had taken shape and held back enough water for the Colonel to decide where he would build the new beaver lodge.

The beaver family rested in their temporary home, the root system of a giant swamp oak that the rushing water had exposed.

Malachi and B'rats began their day searching for berries and nuts. They also gathered dried leaves and grasses and placed them in their new home to insulate it against the cold winter weather ahead.

Miss Calley was still asleep when the jays began to sound an alarm.

"Jay, Jay, Jay," shouted the two-feathered lookouts.

A family of coons inspecting the newly constructed dam felt their way toward Miss Calley's den tree.

As Miss Calley lay in her **den**[59], her eyes filled with tears when she heard a familiar voice.

Could it be? she thought. It sure sounded like—"Mamma!" she shouted, rising and peering out her den.

Sure enough, Miss Calley's mother and brothers were busy investigating the newly constructed dam.

Miss Calley scurried head-first down the tree and greeted her family.

"I thought we would never see you again. Where have you been?" asked the excited raccoon.

"After the farmer trapped us in his corn field," Mamma said, "he brought us to this place and released us. This is the most beautiful home in the world. My, you sure have grown, Calley. Are you okay?"

"If it weren't for my friends Malachi, B'rats, Ruckus, Douglas, Slick, and the Paddlewackers, I would never have found you. I'll tell you all about them while we fish for crawfish. By the way, frogs are not on the menu at this beaver pond," advised Miss Calley as she ambled down to the water.

Awakened from a nap by the sounds of chattering and purring raccoons, Malachi and B'rats looked out of their new home to see Miss Calley and her family.

"Would you look at that, B'rats?" said Malachi. "Miss Calley has found her family".

"Malachi, do you ever miss our home in the city?" asked B'rats.

"Every once in a while," Malachi said. "I miss the sounds and

---

[59] **Den** – a wild animals home. *Example : The Raccoon made her den in a cavity at the top of the hollow tree.*

smells of the city. Especially, Mr. Fipples Fish Market and the bakery next door. They sure had great garbage."

"Do you remember the first time we met?" asked B'rats.

"I sure do. We were on that alley cat's dinner menu," said Malachi.

"It seems like we are always on somebody's dinner menu," said the frazzled rat. "Speaking of food, where is our—?"

"In-coming," shouted Slick as Douglas delivered the first course of the morning's breakfast."

Malachi and B'rats dashed into the door of their new home, and as usual, not all of B'rats was safe inside.

"Oooooouuuuch, my tail, my precious tail," shouted B'rats. "The things I have to put up with. I don't know which is worse, a hungry alley cat or a know-it-all blue jay that drops breakfast from fifty feet."

Each night the beaver dam grew and grew until it was finally finished. As the small community of animals looked about them, they were content in the new habitat they had made.

Malachi and B'rats had a home without the hustle and bustle of city life. Miss Calley and Ruckus had their own coon-dominium that was large enough to raise a family. The Paddlewackers had a beautiful new lodge and a strong dam that would hold back enough water to supply all the animals in the forest, and it was equipped with their very own Skeeter Eater.

As the beavers put the finishing touches on their lodge, Fidget, Furfit, and Fret swam to the beaver dam and erected the flat brown board that ensured the animals the natural habitat was their special place—a small place on a big planet left just for the plants and animals.

Malachi sighed softly.

"Isn't life in the Refuge great?"

About the author

Lucy Johnston Moreland was raised on a small farm in rural central Arkansas. As she grew up, the outdoors, nature, and working with animals was part of her everyday life. As an adult, her career has consisted of educating people about wildlife, the environment, conservation, and the wise use of our natural resources. Over the past 30 years, Lucy has served as Executive Director of the Arkansas Wildlife Federation, 4-H Conservation Education Program Coordinator for the University of Arkansas Cooperative Extension Service, and Chief of Education Division for the Arkansas Game and Fish Commission.

As a Wildlife Rehabilitator, Lucy has raised numerous species of orphaned or injured animals. These animals have been used to educate thousands of individuals about wildlife and our natural resources.

Now retired, she enjoys her grandchildren, wildlife watching, canoeing, fishing/hunting, hiking and cooking. Most of all she still enjoys educating children about our natural resources.

About the Illustrator

Robin Apple, a country girl at heart, grew up in Pensacola, Florida and in small town Dardanelle, Arkansas. She spent her college years in Arkansas learning about art and studying the biological sciences. A love of animals inspired her to express her affection through her art.

TEXALINA PRESS

TEXAS

ARKANSAS

64007630R00076

Made in the USA
Lexington, KY
24 May 2017